The
Penguin
Games

Nicole Reineke

First paperback edition December 2024
Second paperback edition January 2025

Book design by Nicole Reineke

ISBN 979-8-3001-9937-1(paperback)
Independently published

The Penguin Games

Nicole Reineke

Introduction

Most people slowly creep toward death, their decisions small nudges in determining their method of demise. Years of sitting with crouched shoulders and staring at blue-lit screens inch them toward immobility, which becomes a slow and silent assassin. Decades of repressed anger raise their blood pressure until an aorta bursts during a peaceful morning walk. Or the slow, stubborn neglect of personal ties unspools into lonely, irreversible isolation.

Few set off a series of events that so directly lead to their untimely death as Stella Everdeen. She wasn't drifting or nudging her way toward death. No, she set her course like a captain steering a ship straight into the storm.

Chapter 1

It was the beginning of the New England season when the cornstalks ceased to whisper. The green had surrendered to brittle brown, and the fields no longer swayed but rattled as if caught in the grips of some hidden tremor. To the left, the stalks; to the right, the woods hummed with the low, pulsing energy of massive beehives, the insects busily preparing for the coming frost.

Stella patted her pocket, feeling the familiar shape of the EpiPen and, just below it, the small canister of mace. Six years on this trail and not a single sting, but she wasn't one to take chances. The mace was more of an afterthought, a habit she'd never quite shaken. As a tall former athlete, she liked to think she could outrun most of the people she might cross paths with. But, as she edged toward fifty, she was pretty sure nobody was too interested in kidnapping her. Honestly, since she'd let her curls go gray and her green eyes had developed crow's feet, most people barely noticed her at all.

With a whistle, she called her Old English sheepdog, Finnick, to her side and set out into the back fields. This was their daily ritual, the rhythm of their hikes as constant and grounding as the land itself.

Her earbuds firmly in place, she dialed into the meeting, barely registering the monotonous drone of her coworkers on yet another conference call. She often wondered what would happen if she began each call with the truth: "We're all going to be laid off or dead soon. Is what you're about to say worth it?" She smirked at the thought. She doubted it would go over well with the boss. And she liked this job, so today she remained quiet.

Finnick pulled at the leash, his long, grey, shaggy body rushing forward on his usual mission to nowhere in particular. When Finnick stopped tugging, Stella knew that meant someone was up ahead. She was used to sharing the path with Alice, her neighbor who owned the farm the path ran through. Sometimes, she ran into birdwatchers, aiming their binoculars into the woods in search of the elusive Connecticut warbler. When the small, yellow-bellied bird crossed their sights, it often elicited a few reverent gasps.

She urged Finnick forward. Just around the bend, a couple in their late 60s were dressed as if emerging from the outback. A man and a woman in head-to-toe Patagonia khaki emerged, complete with head nets.

"Nice day for birdwatching," Stella said as she passed by. "Have you seen the warbler?"

"No birds with the GISS of warblers," the woman had the shaky sound of unused vocal cords. "All sightings have been of LBBs consistent with the general appearance of crows."

Stella smiled, her eyes crinkling at the corners. She used to think that only the technology industry insisted on the acronyms that made the world feel like outsiders. Only when she began her daily field walks in 2020 and ran into the birdwatchers did she find a group even more insistent on shortening even the most basic phrases. Imagine her embarrassment when she looked up what birdwatchers meant when they said the acronym GISS (which is phonetically said with a soft "g" sound, like in the word "giant.") After a few false starts, she was able to determine that it meant General Impression of Size and Shape - in the case of the Connecticut warbler, they were looking for small, compact bodies, slender bills, and active, flitting movements. LBBs had been easier to figure out from context. Large Black Birds.

Acronyms. There was something about them that always set Stella's teeth on edge. They were like in-crowd handshakes that people threw around in meetings, trying to prove how much more they knew than everyone else. "We need to integrate the ML model with the API, and don't forget the ROI on the AI stack," they'd say, as if everyone around them was automatically in on the meanings. But the habit wasn't helpful or clever. It was just... exclusionary.

She knew why people used acronyms. Acronyms made things feel official, wrapped up in neat little packages created by some insider club. Tossing out a quick "LLM" or "GPT" gave the speaker a feeling of intelligence and authority. They thought the room would take them more seriously if they tossed out enough acronyms. But in doing that, they shut out anyone who wasn't fluent in their special language. It was as if they were drawing an invisible line between the ones who "get it" and the ones who don't.

Stella hated that. She hated how it made smart people feel small and how it stopped good conversations before they could even begin. It kept people out when the whole point of science and technology was to invite people in, to make the complex simple enough for everyone to understand. So, whenever she heard another acronym casually tossed around, she fought the urge to roll her eyes and made a mental note to spell things out herself. At least then, she thought, we might have a conversation that included everyone.

"Come on Finnick," Stella was eager to get back to her project.

Chapter 2

In her home office, Stella was surrounded by giant monitors full of penguin images; the National Scientific project was a highlight of her day. As an artificial intelligence researcher and developer at Led AI Technologies (which the marketing team insisted on calling LAT), she typically designed and built deep learning models for IT systems, making sure the servers that ran the largest companies in the world were not vulnerable to attacks from hackers. She spent her days training models to find new patterns in data that identified signs of danger. Where were logins coming from? What do users typically click when they sign in? "Big Brother" monitoring was built into the licensing agreements, and it was her job to leverage the data. Her goal was to give her teams a millisecond head start on the bad guys and stop attacks.

But, that is not what would lead to her demise.

Today, she earned her living by playing with machine learning and image detection algorithms to count the number of unique penguin faces. Convincing LAT to sponsor the National Scientific Antarctica expedition was a stroke of brilliance and a welcome change of pace.

But, this penguin project set off an unfortunate chain of events.

Stella's attention had always gravitated toward the improbable. Sure, she shared the tech world's fascination with AI and its potential to transform industries. But Stella thrived on pushing artificial intelligence in unexpected directions, harnessing its capabilities to tread the line between brilliant and absurd. She was driven by a simple belief: to leave the world just a little better than she'd found it. And she had an enduring commitment to protect those who couldn't protect themselves.

Two decades ago, *March of the Penguins* hit the big screen, and Stella was captivated by the emperor penguins braving the harsh Antarctic landscape to raise their young. She could still hear Morgan Freeman narrating, "In the harshest place on Earth, love finds a way." Few animals tugged at her heartstrings like penguins did. Their quirky personalities, fierce family bonds, and resilience in a brutal climate made them creatures she felt compelled to defend.

Working with National Scientific had been a dream she'd carried with her since watching that movie. Knowing that her software would soon be in Antarctica—tracking penguins across the vast expanse of snow, breaking up the endless white landscape with clusters of waddling birds—felt like a monumental win. The scientists focused on studying microplastics, examining how these tiny pollutants had reached even the Earth's most remote corners. Stella admired their dedication, but for her, something else beckoned.

While the scientists collected soil samples, they'd also install satellite-linked, solar-powered cameras across the tundra to document the project. And that's where Stella's true passion ignited. She connected capturing images of the penguins and her work back home: processing and analyzing endless data streams. What if they didn't just take pictures? What if they could identify, track, and name individual penguins?

This simple yet radical idea took hold. They could use the cameras not only to document but also to create a connection, letting the world into the daily lives of individual penguins. Much like ChildFund's iconic commercials, where a specific child's story helps connect people to a cause, one could "adopt" and follow a specific penguin, sharing its survival story. This project expansion would reach beyond research and data; making people care deeply about a bird on the other side of the world. It could turn statistics on microplastics into a survival story worth sharing and taking part in.

And that, in Stella's eyes, made all the difference.

"The scientists are missing the point," she had argued. "If they want change, we need to start connecting to hearts. People will care more about

Primrose the newly hatched chick choking on plastic than they will care about the soil."

She convinced LAT to let her proceed as long as she finished the plastics algorithms. With a little imagination and some incredible coding, Stella built a machine learning algorithm to identify the impacted penguins themselves.

People may think writing an algorithm to detect an animal is challenging. And it is. But it used to be much more difficult. In the past, if Stella wanted to teach a machine to recognize a penguin, she would have needed to gather hundreds, if not thousands, of images, painstakingly dissect them, label each one by hand, and use them to train a model. Every tiny distinction between one bird and the next would have been a manual process, hours of work that felt like chipping away at a glacier with a teaspoon.

But those days were gone. Now, with so many pre-built, friendly algorithms available at Stella's fingertips, she could just grab an image detection model from an open source website like HuggingFace, where people had already done the hard work of building the foundations. She could feed in old videos of penguins and use unsupervised learning. With this, Stella went from zero software to master penguin inspector by using tools that detected patterns on their own. It was as good as if Stella personally watched the penguins on video, noticing their subtle differences and figuring out who was who just by their markings and quirks. The algorithm could even cluster the penguins by similarities and group them without being told which was which.

Stella had chosen a convolutional neural network, an algorithm particularly good at detecting patterns in images. The network started by finding edges and basic shapes—beak, belly, flippers—and then moved on to more complex features as it worked through the layers. It learned by sorting through piles of penguin data and clustering the birds into species based on the visual features it picked up. It had been a stroke of genius, aided by open source software.

The beauty of these models lies in their adaptability. She could continue feeding them new data, allowing the system to grow smarter with each iteration, refining how it identified penguins, even distinguishing one family from another in the chaos of an Antarctic colony. By adding location and timestamp data, the model could observe the penguins like she did, picking up the details and following their journeys across the icy plains.

Chapter 3

Stella's penguin algorithms became an obsession. They were her link to something alive and enduring, even if they would be running in the freezing isolation of Antarctica. While her life grew increasingly solitary, the digital collection of penguins she was building brought an unexpected sense of connection. This tether kept her grounded in her small, quiet house on the edge of a field.

Stella had always been a puzzle-solver, the kind of person who found comfort and order in numbers. With a math degree and a knack for technology, she'd carved out a solid career in high tech, working her way up in the fast-paced Boston tech scene. She'd married once along the way, though that had ended badly. Since then, Stella guarded her privacy with a ferocity that few truly understand.

Seeking a fresh start and some distance, she'd moved from the pulsing city to rural Massachusetts. The historied farmlands and quiet fields offered her a peace she hadn't known during her marriage. Still, she hadn't anticipated just how *quiet* quiet could be. Her new life was isolated, not only by location but by the absence of social connections. Yet as a natural introvert, she found herself adapting. Work was virtual, and her pup and projects became her children.

Stella didn't just want to count penguins; she wanted to know who each one was. Each penguin gained its own digital identity, mapped and stored by her algorithm, which tracked their distinctive markings and movements. She even programmed the system to use names from *The Hunger Games*, automatically assigning each penguin a name as they were detected. As her algorithms improved, she began to run them against past footage from Antarctic expeditions, slowly bringing each penguin into her digital family.

Stella could hardly contain her excitement. The video was no longer just a mass of indistinguishable creatures on the ice; they were Katniss, Peeta, Effie, and Haymitch waddling across the Antarctic plains with purpose and personality. Stella's face lit up every time she saw the system in action, the little penguins flitting across her screen, their names flashing above their heads, populating her database.

Stella uploaded more and more video footage, adding to the test data. Each new penguin was detected, named, and inserted into the database.

ID	Species	First Detected	LatLong	Name
4223	*Pygoscelis adeliae*	10/23/2026 12:02:12.271	-75.250973,-0.071389	Cornelius.451
4224	*Pygoscelis adeliae*	10/23/2026 12:02:12.275	-75.250973,-0.071389	Gale.451
4225	*Pygoscelis adeliae*	10/23/2026 12:02:12.280	-75.250973,-0.071389	Finnick.451

She optimized the algorithm, and it became even faster, taking only milliseconds to detect and categorize the sweet tuxedoed critters. The software did exactly what she wanted: a unique number ID for easy correlation of the penguins across different data sets, correct identification of the species, and a date-time stamp to know the exact moment of detection, exact location, and names. Glorious names.

In her mild obsession with the project, Stella had watched one too many documentaries about penguins. She knew there were about twelve million penguins in Antarctica at any one time. And not just the same twelve million that can be identified, named, and left to their own devices. Imagine, if you will, that you are a fuzzy, adorable creature with no real defense system other than your sweet dark eyes and webbed feet. You must gather your food from the treacherous waters, which are home to none other than your mortal enemies. Seals, sea lions, sharks, and giant birds all seem to find you tasty. Sure, you could live up to twenty years, but it's unlikely. Less than one in five chicks survives to age one. So, the naming, well, that needed work.

Stella needed a way to make tens of millions of names. Names were powerful and important. They helped connect people emotionally. She determined that she wanted a way to endear the penguins to people around the world by personifying them with relatable names. Because the *The Hunger Games* series had under 100 character names, it was not a good source. Stella needed to find a more scalable method to name the penguins.

Chapter 4

On the top right of the 38-inch curved screen, a face flashed up. Bing, bing. Stella would have been annoyed at being interrupted, but it was Violet. Stella always answered for Violet.

Stella pulled off her glasses and picked up her long-cold oolong tea, wondering how much time had passed since she sat down to review the algorithm test results. She clicked the answer button.

"Hello, Violet," Stella said.

"Oh!" came Violet's surprised voice. Her round, bright face and long, stick-straight brown hair filled the screen.

Olga "Violet" Vasiliev never expected people to answer her calls. "The names aren't working. We have to expand the options. Are we connecting out to the language model, or do we want to choose from a static list?"

Stella let out a laugh. She also lacked the art of small talk, which is why they got along so well. "And this is why you're my favorite."

Out of context, most people would have been taken aback by the wildly random question. But, much like Stella, Violet had only one thing on the brain: penguins.

"Monitoring the test outputs, we've exceeded 97.8% accuracy in identifying individual animals. But the specification was to connect penguins with unique names. I'm not feeling any love for Gale.445, and Gale.451 is not connecting with me on an emotional level." Violet rattled on.

Violet was a coder and user-experience expert. She had studied for years ways to connect humans and computers, and if anyone understood the importance of giving each of these creatures a name, it was her.

"I was leaning toward a large language model to supply the unlimited number of naming options rather than creating a database of names," Stella said, looking out the window as her mind wandered back to her morning walk. "It could solve two problems. It would be able to generate an unlimited number of names, and it would provide a natural language interface to learn about each of the penguins when connected to our backend."

The algorithm she had painstakingly coded was clever, yes, but it was just matching penguins to names from her well-worn *Hunger Games* books. Gale. Katniss. Peeta. But there were only so many names a database could generate before it just added numbers to the end to keep them distinct.

The depersonalization of the penguins would be the project's kiss of death.

That's where the large language models (LLMs) could come in. Stella considered their power at the edge of possibility. LLMs weren't built to regurgitate data. They were trained on vast oceans of text, entire libraries of human thought, language, and creativity. They didn't simply follow patterns; they could bend them, reshape them, and create something startling and new. Trained on billions of data points, they could weave words in a way that made each one feel fresh. For Stella's penguins, it meant limitless identities, not bound by any pre-set list of names. Each bird could have a name as unique as the snowflakes beneath its flippers, an identity drawn from the endless well of human language.

And the beauty wasn't just in the names. The LLMs could talk. Well, not really talk, but could interpret human writing and speech and respond with human language. Not in the clunky, robotic way of the early systems but in the fluid, almost conversational manner that made you forget you were speaking to a machine at all. Stella imagined it: scientists asking, "What's the migration pattern of Peeta?" and getting an answer as natural as if they were asking Stella. Or, "How many penguins did we detect last week?" and the model would sift through the backend, pulling data as if it were flipping through a book. The it would respond with the number. No need for complex commands or technical knowledge. Just ask the question, and the LLM could do the rest.

What made it all so irresistible was the adaptability. LLMs weren't static. They learned, evolved, and shaped themselves to the needs of the moment. As Stella's penguin database expanded, the LLM would keep pace, generating new names without falling into repetition. As users asked more questions, the system would dig deeper, offering insights into behavior, patterns, and anomalies with a simple language interface. The LLM would help Stella creating a living, breathing system, a tool that could evolve right alongside the world it was observing. That was the real magic.

But, the accuracy of the LLMs, even well-controlled ones, is only between 70-90%. This meant that you had to account for up to 30% of the information you got back being wrong or made up. These hallucinations had bitten many of the early adopters. There was the Canadian airline fiasco. They had used an open source LLM, a type of artificial intelligence freely available for public use, to replace their customer service representatives with an AI chatbot. However, this meant the chatbot's performance heavily relied on how well the company implemented and monitored it, as open-source technology's underlying code is openly shared and can be modified and used by anyone. These tools often require customization to meet specific needs In this case, the airline failed to put the right guards in place, and the chatbot erroneously created a bereavement policy-basically lying to a grieving passenger. This created a pubic relations fiasco, and made the company liable for the promised full airfare refund.

"Let's use OpenLLaMA. We can use it offline. It will work when it is on the server even if there is no Internet connection," Violet suggested.

Stella considered the implications. Her agreement with LAT and National Scientific indicated that the code they created should be available to the public to help move all scientific research forward. This meant that whatever code they used must also be available to the public. Using an open source tool instead of writing the code herself would save a lot of time and would meet the needs of the project. Stella came to a decision - it was a good idea.

"We wanted to open source the penguin algorithm anyway, so the licensing works," Stella agreed. "What is the risk profile?"

"The risk is low for both the LLM and open source," Violet responded. "We're just naming penguins. The worst thing that could happen is they had bad naming, duplicates, or maybe offensive words included."

Stella made a note to herself to update the LLM prompt to not use offensive words.

"The risk is high, though," Violet continued. "if image data is stored and includes people's faces. Tha, would be a privacy violation."

Stella nodded, her mind drifting back to her previous work with Violet. They frequently ran through risk analysis exercises, and in any typical scenario involving the collection and storage of human images, privacy concerns would be front and center. Just a few months ago, one of her software vendors had recorded a routine meeting. At the time, Stella hadn't given it a second thought; meetings were often recorded for internal use. But a week later she sat in stunned silence as that same vendor, presenting at a conference, pulled her video up on the big screen to showcase the vendor's new AI feature.

She had felt utterly exposed. Yes, technically the vendor had the right to use the video since she had agreed to be recorded for the meeting. But repurposing that video, without her permission, had blindsided her. It wasn't a legal line crossed; it was a matter of respect. She would never release software that risked capturing people's faces without careful planning and full consent.

But this was Antarctica, she reminded herself. The risk was extremely low that human images would be captured in these images, just vast landscapes and a colony of penguins. For once, the risks seemed refreshingly distant. She was comfortable contributing penguin naming to the open source community.

Open source software was a beautiful, yet messy beast, a lot like that sourdough starter she kept in her fridge, the one she barely had time to feed but couldn't quite bring herself to throw out. Open source worked the same way. Someone, somewhere, had created the original "starter." They'd fed it, nurtured it, carefully mixed the right ingredients of code until it was alive, capable of transforming into something meaningful. And then, like any good baker, they split it off and sent pieces of it out into the world for others to use.

But here's the thing about sourdough and open source. Once it's out there, you have no control over what happens next. One person might care for it just as you did, feeding it regularly and using it to bake perfect, golden-brown loaves. Another might forget about it for a few days, toss in a bit of this or that, and suddenly, it's taken on an entirely different character. And when that person passes it along to someone else, who knows what they'll use it for? You might have set out to bake a simple loaf of bread, but down the line, someone's fermenting the starter into beer.

Community sharing–passing code around, improving it, and experimenting with it–is the heartbeat of open source. Just as the flavors in your bread change subtly depending on where your starter's been and who's handled it, software evolves as more and more developers contribute to it. Sometimes, the transformations are radical, and you end up with something completely different from what you intended. The software you built for writing novels could be adapted by someone else to trick, or catfish, the elderly and steal their life savings.

Stella ended the call with her marching orders in hand. They would copy the open source LLM and bring it into their program. With this, unlimited penguin names would be generated in the database in mere hours. Working with Violet was a gift. Stella loved that kid, well, adult, but at her age, anyone in their 20s was young enough to be her kid.

***

Stella tapped her fingers on the desk, staring at the monitor as the database updates flickered across her screen.

ID	Species	First Detected	LatLong	Name
3642 31	*Eudyptes chrysocome*	11/14/2026 11:41:15.421	-75.250973,-0.071389	Vidhya Thelonious
3642 32	*Eudyptes chrysocome*	11/14/2026 11:41:15.921	-75.250973,-0.071389	James Wanderval e

There would be a slight delay in processing time to obtain the unique names, but it was worth it.

After the database finished updating, Stella started a video call with Violet.

"Are you ready to push this out into the wild?" Stella leaned back in her chair. She eyed Violet, who was furiously typing away, clearly in her zone.

"I'm halfway through the process now," Violet said without looking up. "We're still calling it *The Penguin Games*, right?"

Stella snarfed her tea. "Obviously."

Violet quirked a rare grin. She shared her screen, and the familiar lines of code were visible to Stella. "I've added the README. Nothing fancy, just the basics so the nerds know what to do. Also added the common license, so anybody who uses this has to credit LAT and must contribute their work back to open source. You want to do the honors or should I?"

Stella nodded. These were the terms of the engagement with National Scientific, and they had to be the terms of what she released.

"You do it," Stella picked up her tea and sipped. "I'll just watch and feel proud."

"Sure thing," Violet's fingers flew across the keyboard. "Okay, pushing it to the world ...now." She leaned back and stretched. "And there we go. It's officially out there. *The Penguin Games* is live."

"May the odds be ever in their favor," Stella raised her mug in a remote 'cheer.'

"I give it a week before someone turns it into a pigeon tracker," Violet answered.

Stella shrugged. "Maybe someone will use it to name geese. Either way, it's done. It's officially part of the open-source world."

Violet shook her head. "Yup. Now, let's sit back and watch where the nerds take this one."

Stella knew Violet was not happy about the terms of the engagement. As National Scientific was a publically funded program, the work completed on the project had to be contributed to open source. They had both seen what the nerds did to open source - they took it, modified the work, and used it for their most perverse whims.

But, Stella had agreed to the terms, penguins were not people, and Violet was along for the ride despite her reservations.

Stella whistled for Finnick, hooked him up, and headed out for their afternoon walk in the fields.

Chapter 5

On the other side of the world, Garrett Bauer was adjusting to life as an intern at the Australian Agriculture and Trade Bureau, and for a kid from a small farming town in Illinois, it was both surreal and exhilarating. His first-choice internship had been a dream slot at LAT in Silicon Valley, the kind of cutting-edge research place he'd read about and aspired to since high school. He'd nailed three rounds of interviews, tackled their interactive coding test with a perfect score, and felt certain he'd locked it down. But no offer came.

Garrett, however, wasn't the kind of guy to sit back and place all his bets on scoring that job. He'd lined up a couple of backups, and this job in Australia had been his second choice. It was a chance to take his skills abroad, to push himself further away from the Midwest than he'd ever dreamed possible. His weekends, he figured, would be spent exploring the outback or maybe even hopping over to New Zealand. The Bureau's promise of hands-on work with the latest in data science and AI had sweetened the deal.

Getting this internship hadn't been easy, but Garrett's background in farming had worked in his favor. Growing up, he'd spent summers working on his family's farm, learning the ins and outs of crop rotation, pest control, and machinery maintenance. The skills had become second nature to him, and now, ironically, they'd come full circle to help him land this spot. He knew his parents were proud of him, even if they didn't fully understand what data science or AI were. To them, "computer science" was as exotic as "Australia."

Yet here he was: his straw-colored hair and lanky frame stuffed into a 4x4 gray cubicle, one of many in a row, each barely wide enough to spin a chair, the walls low enough for him to see the heads of other interns and employees popping up like prairie dogs. There was no innovation hub, no futuristic lab like he'd imagined. Just an office with a faded carpet, buzzing fluorescent lights, and the steady hum of old air conditioning.

For Garrett, who'd grown up with wide open skies and fields as far as the eye could see, it was a strange, cramped place. And while he was thrilled to be here, he couldn't help but feel a little homesick. He missed his family, the smell of freshly turned soil, and the steady routine of home. But he wasn't about to let that hold him back. Introverted as he was, he was making an effort with his coworkers, even if they found him a little quiet, a little unconventional. Garrett figured he'd earned this position, and he was determined to make the most of it.

Martin Dempsey, Garrett's manager, occupied the cubicle directly next to his. And while the setup was far from glamorous, Martin's cubicle backed up to a window. This tiny upgrade in status tsaid, "not quite the bottom rung," though nowhere near the closed-door offices of the real decision-makers. They were the ones free to sip their coffee in private, their heads never visible above the walls like their employees in the cubicals. In a place where hierarchy was reflected in seating arrangements, Martin's window view was less a privilege and more a reminder of how far he had yet to climb.

It was January, peak summer in Australia, and Garrett couldn't help but notice the way the sun slanted through Martin's window, casting an unflattering spotlight on his manager. The light outlined Martin's large, translucent ears, his short-sleeved button-down shirt steadily darkening with sweat stains pooling under his arms. Even his thin comb-over wilted in the heat, flattening against his scalp in thin, damp patches. Garrett had a kind of detached sympathy for Martin. It wasn't that he was a bad guy, but Martin had a way of blending into the bureaucracy around him, a cog in a machine that didn't give him any real sway. In Garrett's eyes, Martin's lack of influence made him a fairly unremarkable figure, but he was a good enough manager and, at times, seemed to genuinely want Garrett to succeed.

Today, though, Martin was forcing Garrett to sit through mandatory onboarding training, a thinly veiled exercise in government protocol that neither was particularly invested in. Just a cubicle away, Martin could easily keep an eye on Garrett and made it clear that he expected Garrett to log on and give it his "full attention." Dutifully, Garrett clicked into the Zoom call, watching as a scientist droned on about germination rates, pesticide rotations, and the specifics of genetically modified organism regulations in Australian agriculture. Garrett tried, in that first session a few weeks back, to take it seriously; he'd even brushed his hair and put on a button-down shirt, figuring that someone would care about appearances. But no one had noticed, and after a while, the whole process felt like a box-checking exercise.

This time around, he didn't even bother wiping the Pop-Tart crumbs from his T-shirt. They only needed to see his face on camera to mark him "present" for the training, and it wasn't like anyone would care if he was engaged. In hindsight, though, Garrett's decision to tune out would prove to be a costlier one than he could have anticipated—one that might have saved him from his eventual role in Stella's untimely death.

With the volume on low and the Zoom window minimized, Garrett decided to make better use of his time by diving into something that interested him. He opened his browser to the GitHub page for LAT, his dream company, and eagerly scanned the new open-source repositories. Typing "AI" into the search bar, he quickly pulled up a list of the latest projects, scanning each one with a mix of envy and admiration.

AlexisNova / ai-code-optimizer

BrightMinds / vision-enhancer

DataPulse / analytics-booster

NextGenTech / speech-synthesizer

QuantumForge / image-classifier

NeuralNetic / recommendation-engine

SynapseLogic / language-processor

CortexFlow / data-cleanser

StellaEverdeen / the-penguin-games

VividAI / pattern-recognizer

"The Penguin Games?" Garrett squinted at the screen. Odd name for something coming out of LAT. Garrett had stumbled on a few repositories from *StellaEverdeen* before. She was practically a legend in the field, well-regarded for her sophisticated approaches to security algorithms and time-series analysis. He'd studied her projects more than once, almost like a quiet fan, genuinely impressed by her data chops and her ability to wrangle complex information into something refined and powerful.

So when he spotted *The Penguin Games* in the LAT repository, he couldn't resist taking a closer look. He clicked in, his mouse hovering over the README file. The project description was enticing enough to grab him right away: a neural network designed to pick out individual objects from data in real time. Not just differentiating types but also identifying specific, individual penguins.

And then there was the kicker: the program didn't just identify penguins; it named them.

Garrett squinted, running his finger along the line. "Unique names assigned to each penguin, generated through a large language model." He muttered to himself, his voice thick with skepticism. The whole idea was soft, squishy, humanizing, the kind of thing that would make people coo over a creature on a screen. But AI wasn't supposed to be soft. It was supposed to get things done, crunch data, solve problems, and let humans get on with the important stuff.

This? Garrett shook his head, the smile stretching wider. Assigning names and giving them personalities felt a little too emotional. As if people wanted to make AI into something it wasn't meant to be. For him, AI was a way to automate, streamline, to make repetitive tasks disappear in a few clean lines of code. That's why he'd spent years learning this, why he'd gotten into programming in the first place. He didn't want to play around naming animals as if they were characters in a kid's show, but to harness AI as a tool that served a purpose, making life easier, faster, and more efficient.

When he reached the funding note at the bottom of the README—*National Scientific*—it all clicked. Of course. They'd want people naming penguins, assigning quirky traits and humanlike charm to cold data. This wasn't about AI for efficiency's sake; it was about selling a story, dressing up penguins and humanizing them for public appeal.

He couldn't help but feel a mix of admiration and irritation. Stella was a genius, no question there, but he'd never expected her to be the type to jump on the "humanized AI" bandwagon. He closed the README with a huff, shaking his head. AI, in his opinion, was here to make life smoother, not to give people imaginary friends in Antarctica.

"Automate tasks, get results, move on," he said to no one in particular.

With a glance, he checked the training video on Zoom. The scientist was still droning on, now with an inexplicable slide of a kangaroo beside him. Garrett returned to his browsing.

For his internship, Garrett had been tasked with predicting and normalizing output expectations for local crop production. For days, he sat at his desk, combing through data, matching crop types with actual yield figures. The task boiled down to a simple exercise: take numbers from the database, run basic math, turn it into code, and create a bare-bones interface that would show what farmers had planted versus expected outcomes. The goal was to help the planning teams set more accurate expectations for next season. Anyone with a basic handle on acreage, planting yields, and linear algebra could do it. And so, here he was, wasting his brilliant mind on grade-school farming math.

Garrett had finished his project and submitted the code to Martin the previous week. Martin should have been thrilled. Garrett had delivered everything the department needed for next year's crop planning, complete with calculations and algorithms that could streamline output predictions. But thrilled he was not. Martin hadn't wanted an intern in the first place. An intern came with funding, yes, but funding that his boss could redirect toward other, more pressing projects. Martin had agreed to host a student only because it meant extra resources for the department. And so, Garrett found himself with no new instructions and a lot of free time.

Garrett sat back in his chair, staring at the faint cracks in the ceiling tiles above him. Free time. It was supposed to be a luxury, especially here on the other side of the world, farther than anyone in his family had ever traveled. But instead, it felt like being left out in a field with no map and no compass. He felt the ache of homesickness creeping in, a longing for the Midwest skies, his family's farmhouse, and the way the land stretched wide and open– free from the fabric-sided walls currently corralling him.

Not one to let his mind atrophy, Garrett was determined that this unexpected freedom would work in his favor. He had no intention of putting "calculated crop yield" as the sole bullet point on his summer internship résumé. No, if he was stuck in this intellectual desert, he would take matters into his own hands and pursue something far bigger. Maybe, he mused, he could tackle the problem of food scarcity across Australia by figuring out what is causing lower-than-expected yields. The reasons couldn't be that different than what he saw back home, probably drought or soil content or some regional fungi. The idea thrilled him. That would certainly be worth a mention in the academic journals. Maybe it would even get him on the Forbes "30 Under 30" list.

As soon as the training call ended, Garrett decided to press Martin on his newest idea.

"What are you planning to do with the crop output data?" Garrett asked, peering over the top of the cubicle wall, his voice unfiltered and direct.

Martin rubbed his hands over his deeply lined face, suppressing a sigh. He'd seen this coming. For the past week, Garrett had been gently asking for more work, and Martin had given no thought whatsoever to inventing a new project. The truth was, he had more important things to do, like avoiding everything he possibly could. Avoidance was practically an art form for Martin: avoiding the intern in the cubicle next door, avoiding his boss, whom he hoped would forget he existed, and most of all, avoiding work.

"Nah, it's not my job to do anything with it," Martin replied at last. "It all goes up to the planning board. They're the ones who decide what crops get the funding."

Garrett's nose wrinkled in disbelief. "That doesn't make sense. Why not try to reduce crop loss proactively?"

Martin spun his chair around, reluctantly facing the young man whose curiosity had already become an unwelcome fixture in his day. "I'm sure someone's thought of that, but it's way above my pay grade," he replied, with as much patience as he could muster.

But Garrett's mind was already racing. "What if I set up a regressive root cause analysis?" he suggested. "I could link in all the data sources we have access to and look for correlations with the yield failures."

Martin blinked. He wasn't exactly sure what the kid meant, and it certainly didn't sound like the kind of thing he wanted to deal with. But if it would keep Garrett busy and out of his hair for another week, he was willing to nod along.

"Yeah, ok," Martin said, as casually as possible, before spinning back to his computer screen. As far as he was concerned, the problem was solved.

Chapter 6

Garrett set to work, diving into every dataset the Australian Agriculture and Trade Bureau had to offer in his quest to find the root causes behind crop yield failures. Some of the data was straightforward and available in department-sanctioned datasets. But other parts lay locked behind virtual walls, access limited to more senior personnel. No matter; he slipped around a few digital gates to gain entry, justifying his unauthorized access as a necessity for the greater good—saving crops and, more urgently, alleviating his crushing boredom.

One database held over a century's worth of weather records; another, decades of soil content analyses; and in yet another, readings on fungal presence and infestation levels. As he scrolled through, Garrett shook his head, "No wonder they can't solve their problem. Nothing here is normalized." Data was scattered across different platforms, inconsistently measured, and poorly integrated.

One of the best things about being a genius, Garrett thought to himself, was seeing patterns and connections in data that others missed entirely. But one of the hardest things about being a genius was having to be the one to make these patterns obvious to everyone else, repeatedly having to prove what was so clear to him. He'd learned this lesson over and over, like in math class, when his teachers had failed him for not showing his work even though his answers were right. Or on the debate team, when he'd stated the correct conclusion only to be marked down for not walking the panel through his reasoning.

So he knew he'd have to do more than simply understand the data; he'd need to construct logical, visual connections that would lead the rest of them to see what he already saw, step by painful step.

Initially, Garrett focused on weather patterns, suspecting that drought was the primary culprit behind the low crop yields. He'd seen the news about wildfires and the drying rivers firsthand, the lack of water apparent across some areas of the land. Pulling the historical weather data into a vector database, he normalized the data— essentially smoothing out the chaos. Raw data often came in scattered and inconsistent, like a hundred mismatched jigsaw puzzles thrown together. Normalizing meant reshaping it, aligning each piece so it fit into a coherent picture. For Garrett, that meant converting temperature readings, rainfall amounts, and humidity levels into a uniform format, linking them to specific locations and dates, and cross-referencing it all with crop field coordinates and planting schedules. It wasn't glamorous work, but without it, the data was just noise. Normalization turned the noise into something he could actually use—a framework where patterns might finally reveal themselves. He tried every angle he could think of, grouping by crop types, soil content, fertilizer data, and rainfall patterns.

But analysis after analysis came up short. Beyond the typical fluctuations, there was no clear evidence that drought alone was driving down yields. Frustrated, Garrett shifted his focus to fungus counts, comparing them against crop outputs, expecting to see a significant link. Yet, even with decades of fungal readings, the data didn't match up to the massive crop losses some fields had experienced. Fungus wasn't the smoking gun.

It had to be something else. Pests, perhaps? Garrett pulled pesticide usage records and began plotting these against crop losses. Maybe it was the organic farms, losing yield because they were battling pests with natural solutions instead of chemicals. But here too, he found nothing definitive. Pest patterns and pesticide usage didn't correlate with the drastic losses, either.

Digging deeper, Garrett scoured the network for any obscure or hidden datasets, something overlooked. One particularly slow Tuesday, his exhaustive search finally yielded something unexpected: a dataset titled *Project Fly*. A shiver ran down his spine. Flies, he thought, disgusted. But intrigue got the better of him.

Garrett opened the README file.

Project Fly: Review of 2025 Agricultural Drone Project

Classification: Internal Use Only

March 1, 2025 - Agricultural project utilizing drones—referred to as "Flys"—to enhance crop yields through precision seed distribution.

The drones were designed to fly over designated fields and distribute seeds into the soil at specific depths and intervals, optimizing planting patterns to improve crop productivity.

Technical Specifications:

Drone Capabilities: Each Fly was equipped with high-resolution cameras for field surveillance and navigation.

Seed Distribution Mechanism: A funnel and air-gun assembly was integrated for targeted seed firing, allowing controlled dispersal at calculated depths and spacing.

Operational Control: Drones were remotely piloted by certified operators, ensuring adherence to specific field patterns and safety protocols.

Outcome and Evaluation: Despite initial promise, the project encountered several operational and financial challenges, leading to its discontinuation.

Key issues included:

Cost Inefficiency: The high cost of drone units and certified pilot operators significantly impacted the yield-to-cost ratio, making the program financially unsustainable.

Technical Limitations: The seed distribution system frequently experienced mechanical failures, with the funnel and air-gun mechanisms prone to jamming. This resulted in inconsistent seeding patterns and reduced effectiveness.

Conclusion: Given these challenges, the project was terminated due to an inability to justify further investment. The costs associated with drone operation and maintenance, coupled with mechanical reliability issues, indicated that the technology was not viable for large-scale agricultural deployment under current conditions. Recommendations are underway to assess potential redesigns or alternative solutions for cost-effective

agricultural innovation in future
initiatives.

Action Required: None.

"We have drones?!" Garrett exclaimed.

Martin, who had been quite happily ignoring his intern for the past few weeks, turned around, startled.

"Drones?" Martin asked, his eyes narrowing.

Garrett held up his laptop, practically vibrating with excitement.

"Look, it's all here," Garrett said, marching over to Martin's cubicle. "We've been flying drones over fields to collect data and even trying to use them for planting!"

Martin leaned back instinctively, unused to anyone invading his personal space. But when he caught a glimpse of the drone image on Garrett's screen, his curiosity got the best of him. He leaned forward, brow furrowed.

"Huh. We have drones," Martin said, a glimmer of interest breaking through his usual indifference.

When Garrett stumbled upon the report, his mind made two crucial connections. First, drones and agriculture were actively intersecting in their department. Second, that meant that somewhere there was a record of the fields observed from the sky.

"The numbers alone aren't giving me answers," Garrett explained. "But images might."

Garrett began outlining his thought process. If they could get images across the growing season, they might be able to visually pinpoint the exact stage where the crops started failing. It was a fresh perspective on their problem, one that added a tangible dimension to all the data he'd been sifting through.

One of the benefits of attending a top technical school was access to industry experts. Last semester, Garrett attended a geospatial consortium presentation on satellite imagery and the extensive availability of data from global satellite systems. Nearly every inch of Earth was regularly photographed by orbiting satellites.

As he explained this, Garrett connected the dots out loud. Drones were great, but if they didn't have all the coverage they needed, satellites could fill in the gaps. It was the first time Martin seemed to fully grasp Garrett's potential. And, to Garrett's surprise, he almost looked impressed.

"All right," Martin said, cracking a small, reluctant smile. "Satellite images are our next stop."

Chapter 7

Google Earth Engine, a free scientific platform, offers satellite imagery from every corner of the world, available to anyone curious enough to look. You could type in any location, your childhood neighborhood or a vast Australian farm, and pull up images taken over time, like a digital scrapbook of the earth. Garrett, with his relentless curiosity and plenty of time on his hands, logged in, entered the coordinates of the fields he'd been analyzing, and began exploring the catalog of satellite images available from two primary sources, Landsat and Sentinel.

The satellite images, captured over days, weeks, and years, gave him snapshots of each field's life cycle, one picture after another, revealing how the land changed over time. Each image showed the same field, captured in perfect, crisp detail, enough to reveal every row of planted crops, the texture of the earth, even signs of seasonal shifts. Garrett ensured that the quality of these images would serve his purpose, studying each for the right amount of detail. Fortunately, the images were clear enough that he could see even subtle changes between one capture and the next.

Within hours, Garrett had built a simple program to connect with Google Earth Engine. Using open-source tools as his foundation and adding a few adjustments, he made a system that could pull in the satellite images automatically, retrieving snapshots of the fields he wanted to study and storing them locally on his computer. Now he had what he needed: a complete visual history of the fields over the growing season.

Next, Garrett found an open-source algorithm, something other researchers had developed and freely shared, that could help him compare these images. The algorithm would take each daily or weekly image of a field and analyze it for small changes over time, such as shifts in plant growth patterns, crop health, and other visual markers that might tell the story of why these crops were failing.

Garrett had expected that this historical data would reveal fields that didn't grow properly or crops that gradually withered and died over time. But what he saw was nothing like that. In the images of the high-loss areas, where farmers were losing significant portions of their yield, Garrett had anticipated seeing crops that struggled and slowly faded. Instead, he found a disturbing pattern.

In many of these areas, crops didn't just fade. They were physically crushed. Between one image and the next, vast patches of the field were visibly trampled, entire sections flattened as though something massive had passed through. The crop loss wasn't gradual or subtle; it was stark and sudden. From one moment to the next, healthy fields turned into patches of broken, flattened plants.

For the first time, Garrett felt a shiver of uncertainty. This wasn't the drought, a fungus, or a pest gnawing at the edges of the crops. Something else was at work, and whatever it was, its wake was not subtle.

Garrett scrolled through the images, flipping back and forth between frames until something unusual caught his eye–a grey-brown blur near the edge of one of the fields. In the next image, that exact area had transformed into a patch of trampled land. Intrigued, he zoomed in, increasing the resolution bit by bit until the shape became unmistakable: two large hind legs and a long, muscular tail.

Kangaroos. Specifically, the western gray kangaroo is one of Australia's most common (and most troublesome) species.

Now, if Garrett had paid attention during his training calls, he might have known that the Agriculture and Trade Bureau had already analyzed causes of crop loss, with the kangaroo destruction ranking high on the list. Kangaroos, it turns out, are classified as "impact-causing species." And for good reason. With their grazing and relentless foot traffic, they left whole fields ravaged in a matter of days, their massive footprints marking every square foot of flattened crops.

The western gray kangaroo was well-known among Australian farmers for its destructive habits. This species had been the nemesis of crops across the region, with farmers resorting to costly fencing and tree guards to keep them at bay. But fencing often wasn't a perfect solution. Kangaroos, as you know, can jump, *very* high, rendering most fences laughably ineffective. And the numbers weren't in the farmers' favor, either. In the Hills and Fleurieu region alone, 47,000 western gray kangaroos feed and trample their way across the landscape.

But enough about kangaroos. This story is about Garrett and his role in Stella's ultimate demise.

He looked up from his laptop, eager to tell Martin about his discovery, only to realize that the office was dark, the cubicles empty. It was well past closing time. The realization that kangaroos were the hidden culprits didn't just light a spark—it ignited a wildfire of thought that refused to be contained. Garrett's mind raced with possibilities, plans, and half-formed ideas, all demanding his immediate attention.

By the time he left the office, the world outside felt distant, as if his thoughts had created their own bubble around him. He barely noticed the walk home, consumed by the nagging feeling that he was onto something big. His cramped studio apartment greeted him like an extension of his focus, its cluttered chaos the perfect reflection of his mental state.

Chapter 8

Garrett returned to the kind of place that barely qualified as livable but fit snugly into his intern budget. It was a cramped studio, complete with a hot plate for a "kitchen" and paint peeling from the walls. He had space for a couch or a bed, but certainly not both. He'd opted for neither and instead camped out nightly on a blowup mattress wedged between his 48-inch TV, which came with the let, an X-box, which came in his luggage, and a small pile of books he'd picked up at the thrift shop. Yet tonight, none of that mattered—his mind was already working through the night's next steps.

After microwaving a bowl of ramen noodles, he dropped onto the edge of his mattress, put on his gaming headset, and booted up *theHunter: Call of the Wild*, his latest digital obsession. In the immersive hunting simulation, Garrett could lose himself for hours tracking prey. He scanned for footprints, noted subtle disturbances in the ground cover, mapped out watering holes and carefully considered the wind patterns. It was all about strategy and precision, and when he finally locked in on the buck's path, he would spend another hour meticulously selecting the perfect weapon to take down his target. His eyes narrowed, he aimed, held his breath, and, *click*, the deer was his.

It was then, in that quiet, triumphant moment, that another spark flickered in his mind. Kangaroos, he thought. They, too, were creatures that could be tracked, mapped, and even hunted. Why not?

His heart picked up speed. Wide-eyed, he ripped off his headset, ramen forgotten, and scrambled for his backpack, pulling out his laptop with an urgency he hadn't felt in weeks. He was familiar with moments of sudden, electric clarity. His mother often referred to them as glimpses of genius. Garrett's stomach clenched as a wave of homesickness washed over him.He opened Draw.io, the simple workflow tool he used for projects. Garrett began to sketch his vision. Each box and arrow represented a piece of his new plan, the flow taking shape as he outlined the steps:

1. Satellites capture the general field.
2. Satellite images are analyzed to direct drones to general areas of interest.
3. Drones capture live footage over fields.
4. Images are processed onboard the drones, using compact processors like Raspberry Pi.
5. Image recognition software identifies any kangaroo spotted in the fields.
6. Direction analysis determines if the kangaroo is moving toward or away from the crops.

Garrett's mind raced with the potential. He wasn't just creating a solution; he was inventing an entirely new way to control pests–A way that didn't require fences or tree guards. He stared at the workflow. He had identified the pests, but how could he prevent crop destruction?

Garrett knew he couldn't deploy armed drones. He was tempted, sure, but hunting kangaroos came with ethical and logistical challenges. He'd taken an entire course in AI ethics, and killing people or animals with drones was right at the top of the list of civilian no-gos. Besides, his manager already didn't seem thrilled with him; proposing kangaroo-hunting drones would probably not help his case. It might even get him labeled as a psychopath. But Garrett had another idea.

Growing up, his family had spent time camping. One of the first things they'd learned for "wildlife safety" was the power of air horns, essential tools to keep coyotes and bears at bay. The loud blasts were usually enough to scare off anything within earshot. Garrett reasoned that if air horns worked for coyotes, they'd likely work on kangaroos, too. Equipping drones with air horns could turn them into mobile scarecrows, driving the kangaroos away from the crops to feed elsewhere.

He picked up his phone and looked at the time: midnight. It would be 1 PM back home.

Garrett: would air horns scare off kangaroos
Mom: They scared the crap out of your dad, so yes. They would probably shake up a kangaroo ☺
Garrett: hehe

Mom: Don't hike alone
Garrett: no, for drones
Mom: Drones aren't afraid of noise
Garrett: smh I think kangaroos are wrecking crops
Mom: Ahhh. Remember the coyotes? Most of them
wouldn't come near us after we used the air horns.
Except that big one kept coming back until we
brought out the shotgun
Garrett: got it
Garrett: need a plan for repeat offenders. luv ya
Mom: I love you too. Make good choices. Can't wait
for you to be home

Garrett updated his design:

- Drone identifies the kangaroo.
- If new, and headed toward the crops, initiate air horn.
- If repeat kangaroo and headed toward the crop, notify system for human intervention.

The workflow was elegant, simple, and straightforward: detect the kangaroos, add them to a database, intervene, and notify. His brain clicked to the project that had dropped from LAT weeks ago.

"The Penguin Games," he cheered to himself, beaming at the screen. Stella Everdeen had posted an entire open-source system that handled animal identification, naming, and location tracking. He'd have to tweak the image recognition to focus on kangaroos and add drone integration for directional tracking. With this setup, he was halfway there.

Garrett was going to be a hero to farmers everywhere. "Do they give Nobel prizes to software engineers?" he wondered, half-joking, half-hopeful. Now *this* was work worth doing.

Eager to get started, Garrett navigated to GitHub and branched *the-penguin-games* repository, setting up his local development environment with a smirk as he named the branch GH-KH. Garrett Harrison - Kangaroo Hunter. He liked the sound of that.

Garrett looked up the documentation for the drones mentioned in the *Fly Project*. With any luck, he figured the Australian government had those sitting in storage somewhere, unused. As he scanned through the specifications, something caught his eye: the drones already had built-in speakers and could play audio files. It was perfect. By the time the sun started to rise, Garrett had everything he needed—simulation data for kangaroo identification, a way to register each kangaroo (names included; he hadn't bothered removing that feature), a "first offense" sound blast to scare off newcomers, and a notification system that could send farmers a text with the exact location of any repeat offender showed up and didn't back down.

When his alarm went off to head to work, Garrett was startled. For the first time that summer, he called in sick. Instead of crashing into bed, he grabbed a Pop-Tart, sat back down at his laptop, and dug into his code, refining his program with fresh determination.

As the sun dipped below the horizon, casting the room in a faint orange glow, Garrett shoved aside a pile of crumpled Pop-Tart wrappers. He barely registered the empty box; his mind was wholly consumed by his project. After hours of coding and endless lines of logic, the program still wasn't working as it should.

He leaned back, rubbing his temples, staring at the screen as if sheer willpower could force the code to cooperate. Everything was set up, and every component was connected. The image recognition was trained, the drone integrated, and the notification system primed. By all rights, it *should* have been working. But it wasn't.

Somewhere in his code, a single flaw lurked, keeping his grand plan from coming to life.

ID	Species	First Detected	LatLong	Name
642	*Macropus fuliginosus*	1/12/2027 13:32:12.076	-31.5000,138.5000	Dundee June
643	*Macropus fuliginosus*	1/12/2027 13:32:32.472	-31.5000,138.5000	Rachelle Zane

The accuracy of Garrett's image recognition algorithm stubbornly hovered at 70%, identifying kangaroos as various other animals. He double-checked the footage labeled *Billie Haliway*, a name assigned to a particularly elusive kangaroo. Not a dog, he thought, scrutinizing the shape on his screen. But the drone footage wasn't crisp; the images were captured from above, a tricky angle that traditional image recognition models, built mostly for ground-level photos, weren't designed to handle. From this height, the animal looked slightly distorted. He could see why the algorithm was confused; in the overhead shot, Billie's hunched posture and shadow cast a silhouette that resembled a large grey dog.

He needed more than a few tweaks; he needed a breakthrough. Taking a deep breath, Garrett minimized his code editor and opened his browser. He navigated back to GitHub, searching for the project he'd forked the night before: *the-penguin-games*. Stella Everdeen's work was nothing short of genius in Garrett's eyes. She'd designed her model to identify and track penguins, even in clusters, on vast snowfields. Her system could detect subtle details and learn as it went, becoming more accurate with every frame. Surely, she'd solved the same types of issues he was facing now. If her model could master penguins in snow, there had to be a way for his to handle kangaroos in the outback.

Garrett pushed his code updates to his GitHub repository, the folder where the files are stored, GH-KH, ensuring everything was clean and well-documented. Then he navigated to the private messaging section, his fingers hovering over the keyboard as he gathered his thoughts. Finally, he began to type out his plea for help:

Hey @StellaEverdeen! I'm working with the Agriculture and Trade Bureau in Australia and tweaked your penguin ID model to spot kangaroos from overhead drone shots. It's kinda working, but I'm stuck at like 70% accuracy. Using unsupervised learning here, but the top-down view is messing with the model-keeps tagging kangas as dogs. Any tips on boosting accuracy with these weird angles or adding in movement patterns? Thx a ton!

Garrett hit "Send." He knew it might be a while before she replied, if she chose to at all. Stella was a legend in the open-source community, but she was also busy, probably off working on some high-level project that went over most people's heads. Still, he held out hope. Maybe she'd recognize the potential in his problem. Maybe, just maybe, she'd have the insight he needed to push his model past that stubborn 70% accuracy.

With a flicker of renewed optimism, Garrett shut his laptop, stretched out on his air mattress, and finally closed his eyes. Within moments, exhaustion took over, and he drifted off, sleeping soundly for the first time in two days.

Chapter 9

Violet tugged at the zipper of her dark blue LAT hoodie, noticing that her current sweats were also branded with the LAT logo. She paused, wondering if she even owned clothing that wasn't emblazoned with her employer's branding. It had been a long time since she'd gone anywhere other than her home office, the supermarket, or the gym.

Her thoughts were interrupted by a ping from her screen. A new notification had appeared in the penguin-games repository: an update on a branch labeled GH-KH from user @garrett_bauer. Curiosity sparked, and she clicked the alert. It was their first official fork—a milestone. Someone was using their code to create something new.

As she scrolled through the changes, she took note of the comments left by @garrett_bauer in the code, her interest growing with each line.

"Drone-based kangaroo tracking for crop protection," she whispered, eyebrows raised."Australian Agriculture and Trade Bureau?" As she reviewed the code, she felt that Garrett's modifications were technically sound and clever. He'd managed to integrate the image recognition software with the drone API, extending the front end to interpret the live feed.

Violet knew Stella would want to see this. It had only been a few weeks since they'd released their code, and someone had branched it in such an unexpected direction. Within minutes, she and Stella were on a video call, poring over the branch like it was some kind of digital treasure map.

"Look at this," Violet said, sharing her screen. "He's trying to refine the image intake in the function Kang_RFM, but he's hitting a wall with the accuracy. Ugh, we need to give this nerd a lesson in naming and code commenting. No one knows what "RFM" stands for. I think the model's struggling to distinguish kangaroos from the background noise in the overhead shots. The footage is throwing off the pattern detection."

Stella's face got larger on Violet's screen as Stella leaned closer to her camera, her expression thoughtful. "He's on the right track, but he's missing something in the preprocessing. We need to adjust the image intake to normalize the backgrounds better before the images are run through the classifier. Let's give him a nudge."

Violet heard the keys clacking as Stella logged into GitHub.

"Look at that, a message from Garrett. He knows he's stuck," Stella said.

With a grin, Violet and Stella dove into the code, focused on refining the image processing pipeline to handle the challenging conditions of the Australian terrain. They adjusted the contrast and brightness thresholds, fine-tuning the model to distinguish subtle shifts in kangaroo shadows against rocky ground. Stella nudged the algorithm to filter out anything resembling a dog and reinforce kangaroo identification. Violet even pushed a small update to the front-end drone interface, giving Garrett's model access to extra data from the drones, including altitude, speed, and wind direction. These elements would help the algorithm sharpen its predictions and accuracy.

In a few hours, their changes were ready to be merged into *the-penguin-games* and then pulled into Garrett's program, GH-KH. Violet clicked to initiate the merge, watching the lines of code blend together. But as they fused, a chill settled over her. A dark thought crept in, one she couldn't shake. She turned back to the camera, her voice quiet but laced with unease.

"Stella, do you realize how close this is to becoming a military surveillance tool? The way Garrett's integrated this with drone technology…. It wouldn't take much for someone to adapt it. This could go beyond animal tracking fast, and there are people out there who wouldn't hesitate to use it that way."

Violet's face grew hot. She grew up in a country where surveillance was woven into the fabric of daily life, but not in the innocuous, neighborhood-watch kind of way. No, this was a kind of watching that made you think twice before saying anything, before sharing too much, before letting anyone see too deep. It was a place where the data they gathered on you could decide your future. By the time she was old enough to realize what was happening, Violet had become accustomed to the faint hum of distrust that underscored her every action.

Living under constant observation, Violet felt even the smallest decisions could be quiet rebellions. Growing up, she had watched neighbors disappear and careers destroyed over an action that didn't align with the prevailing agenda. Data was powerful and, in the wrong hands, it was lethal. Violet knew this in her bones, in the cautious way she moved through the world, always aware of who was watching. It was why she'd chosen to work in tech—to understand the mechanics behind the system, to see the monster up close.

Now, here she was, staring at lines of code that could open the same doors she'd spent her life closing. Stella saw a way to protect penguins, a charming, almost innocent mission to humanize these animals and tell their stories to the world. But Violet knew the darker side, knew how fast the lines blurred when tracking entered the picture. One tweak, one misused line of code, and this wouldn't just be about nature preservation anymore. It could become something far more sinister.

Her fingers hovered over the keyboard as her mind raced through the implications. She imagined someone with less scruples, someone in power, leveraging this technology to monitor individuals, tracking their every move under the guise of "safety." She pictured a person labeled as a "repeat offender" because they'd walked through a field too many times, only now it was a city, a town square, someone's home.

"Stella, we can't let this out," Violet said softly, the urgency of her past coloring her voice.

They sat in silence, the weight of her words settling over them. It was easy to get caught up in the elegance of a solution, to see it as just lines of code, a new problem solved. But this wasn't just code. It was something that could be twisted into a tool for surveillance, for monitoring, for control. Yes, for crops now, but what next? Things neither of them wanted to be responsible for unleashing. A few more tweaks, a few people creating a few more branches, and suddenly, it would not be about animals anymore. It could go from the original intent to save the emperor penguin families to tracking people, and that was a line they'd never meant to cross.

"Violet, software already tracks people. We aren't creating anything that doesn't already exist," Stella said quietly. "I'll add the license restrictions to make clear that this code is not to be used for military applications."

Violet watched the shared screen as Stella updated the license document on "The Penguin Games", each line appearing in the shared project log like a quiet but forceful stand. Violet's stomach twisted with a familiar sense of foreboding as she read through Stella's new restrictions: no military use, no human surveillance applications, and certainly no weapons integration. Human tracking was an absolute no-go. The lines were bold and clear. They were intended to cut off any potential for misuse.

But Violet knew all too well how licenses were ignored. The simplest intentions could be warped once software was released into the wild. She hovered her mouse over Stella's notification, watching as it was dispatched to their follower list:

Attention to all viewers of "The Penguin Games" repository:

Recent updates include new restrictions on the use of this software. Please review the updated license to ensure compliance. This software is intended strictly for environmental monitoring and conservation efforts, not for military or security applications.

Violet leaned back, her gaze drifting to the corner of her screen, where Stella's notification had been sent into the ether. It was strange how a few words on a license could feel so hollow when she thought about the stakes. The real risks happened beyond the neat confines of code and licenses. Knowing the intricacies of the code, Violet felt the thin layer of control slipping from their hands. She felt a twinge of doubt, something Stella probably hadn't let herself linger on; or if she had, had kept well-hidden.

For a moment, Violet's stared into the grayness outside her window. She wanted to believe this licensing update was enough, that words and boundaries could keep the project safe. But in the back of her mind, a voice whispered that it might only be a matter of time before someone ignored the rules, a matter of when, not if.

Chapter 10

Alice Chan leaned against the kitchen counter, staring out at the fields beyond. The sunlight was trying its hardest to make those brown, brittle cornstalks look picturesque, casting a warm glow over what was, in truth, a wasteland. But she wasn't fooled. Her cornfield, her great adventure, was a mess. When she'd first bought the land, she'd thought growing food would be a natural extension of her skills. After all, she had two master's degrees and a PhD in Computer Science. How hard could growing corn be after decades of balancing network loads and routing protocols?

It turns out that growing corn was harder than coding. Much harder. Farming was unforgiving. And in farming, unlike coding, you couldn't just rewrite the problem away and recompile. You lost a crop early on and you lost an entire year of revenue. She had done well in high-tech. Years of climbing the corporate ladder and receiving stock option grants had enabled her to retire early and buy her New England dream farm, complete with stone walls and rocky, unforgiving soil. But she was unused to failure. And in her eyes, not producing crops and revenue in the first three years was failure.

The kitchen floor creaked beneath her feet, the only sound besides the hum of the fridge. Her husband, Paul, was out mending fences somewhere along the far side of the property, and her son was at school, no doubt plotting his next soccer game strategy with friends.

Alice took a long sip of her coffee, her gaze shifting back to the ragged rows. Last year, it had been root rot, her plants drowning in the record rains that had pooled around their roots, slowly suffocating them. This year, the pests had taken over, as if the universe couldn't wait to throw the next disaster her way. Rabbits and groundhogs came first, munching the tender shoots before she even had a chance to feel proud of their growth. But the worst by far were the crows. Those sharp-beaked, beady-eyed intruders swooped in like a dark wave, pecking away at the delicate new growth until only the battered stubs remained. A murder of crows, appropriately named, perched along her fence line, cawing in the harsh, grating voices that seemed to laugh at her every effort.

Alice had tried all of the natural deterrents. Flannel-shirted scarecrows slumped in the field like silent guardians, aluminum pie tins clattered in the breeze, and even a series of plastic owls stared wide-eyed from atop metal stakes. But a fierce wind had come through last week and toppled it all, and now it lay scattered on the ground, looking as defeated as she felt. Nothing worked. The crows just sneered and returned, undeterred by her defenses.

If she was being honest with herself, the lack of corn and muddy fields was starting to sting. Alice had never been bad at anything before. She'd built systems from scratch, managed entire data networks, and solved technical crises others had deemed impossible. And yet, here she was, beaten by crows.

In spite of her disillusionment with the industry, Alice sometimes missed the tech world she'd left. The efficiency, logic, and predictability of code were comfort comforting. Sure, there had been more than enough dysfunctional personalities and those endless meetings, and entirely too many people threatened by her intelligence, but at least the systems themselves made sense. Code followed rules, logic was stable, and errors could be debugged. The same couldn't be said for a New England summer or the merciless whims of wildlife. A few months ago, she'd begun opening her laptop again, re-immersing herself in the open-source community. She'd told herself it was to keep her mind sharp. It felt good to write a few lines without the pressure of quarterly earnings looming over her head, to dive into digital puzzles where outcomes were under her control.

She pulled her laptop off the kitchen table and checked her email. She saw a new notification—an update from Stella Everdeen on one of her projects. Alice smiled. Stella was her neighbor, living just a few miles down the road, and they'd met by chance on one of Alice's afternoon walks through the fields. An easy camaraderie had formed between them; neither were small-talk types, both more comfortable in the clear-cut world of data than in the uncertain terrain of idle conversation. They shared something rare: lives balanced between the digital world and the love of nature.

Alice opened the email titled *The Penguin Games*. "Not for military use," she noted, surprised. What kind of project was Stella working on that needed such a restriction? She opened the README file.

README: The Penguin Games

//The Penguin Games: Image Recognition for Conservation

Welcome to The Penguin Games, an open-source project dedicated to the identification, tracking, and cataloging of Antarctic penguins to support conservation efforts. This repository provides a fully functional AI model for penguin detection, identification, and location tagging, with a growing toolkit for broader environmental monitoring via drones and satellite imaging. Funding and resourcing are provided by LAT, in

//Project Overview

The Penguin Games began with a straightforward mission: identify individual penguins within colony footage. Using neural networks trained to recognize penguin-specific characteristics, the model accomplishes a variety of tasks essential for researchers and conservationists. Version 1 includes core functions for penguin tracking and data collection, with new updates now allowing inputs from both drones and satellite sources to extend the technology's scope beyond ground-level tracking.

//Core Features - Version 1

//Penguin Identification and Unique Classification

- Identification: Using state-of-the-art image recognition, the model can detect individual penguins within high-resolution footage and still images, recognizing unique physical characteristics to distinguish individuals.

- Unique Naming: Each detected penguin is assigned a unique identifier (drawn from a large language model's name database), allowing researchers to track individual behaviors, interactions, and movements within and across colonies.

//// Location Tracking

- Geo-Tagging: Each penguin sighting includes precise Global Positioning System coordinates based on image metadata. This data allows conservationists to monitor colony distribution and migration patterns.

- Timestamped Data: A date-time stamp accompanies each detection, ensuring chronological tracking of penguin movements and colony dynamics.

//// Data Collection and Management

- Automated Data Logging: The system logs all identified penguins into a structured database, maintaining individual histories for long-term analysis.

- Data Outputs: Users can export detection logs, names, timestamps, and locations for external research and reporting needs.

/// New Features - Version 2

The Penguin Games has now evolved to include Version 2 capabilities, which extend data inputs beyond ground-level footage to enable aerial tracking and monitoring. These updates make it possible to cover large land masses, especially remote areas where environmental data is critical. Merged from GH_KH--a crop monitoring branch by @garrett_bauer of the Australian Agriculture and Trade Bureau.

//// Drone Integration

- Automated Scanning and Detection: With drone integration, The Penguin Games can now detect and identify penguins (and other environmental markers) in real-time from aerial footage.

- Immediate Geo-Tagging and Timestamping:
Drone footage provides enhanced geo-
tagging precision and timestamping
directly within the model, making data
collection even more accurate.

//// Satellite Image Integration

- Broad-Scale Environmental Monitoring:
Satellite inputs offer the ability to
track entire regions over time, capturing
data from remote colonies and shifting
ice patterns. This data can now be
processed directly by the model to detect
penguin colony spread, habitat changes,
and seasonal movement trends.

- Automated Alerts and Event Detection:
The model includes automated event
detection (e.g., detected registered
animal) based on image, allowing for
proactive measures.

/// Licensing and Use

The Penguin Games is a tool created for
conservation and environmental monitoring

efforts only. To ensure responsible use,
Version 2 includes a licensing update:

- No Military or Security Surveillance:
This software is strictly prohibited for
use in military applications,
surveillance, or tracking human activity.

- No Weapon Integration: The code must
not be altered or used to integrate
weaponized systems.

- Environmental and Conservation Use
Only: All data should be collected,
analyzed, and deployed solely for
conservation research and environmental
monitoring.

Please review the full LICENSE.md for
complete terms and conditions.

/// Getting Started

For setup instructions, installation requirements, and user guides, see the INSTALL.md and USER_GUIDE.md in the repository. The Penguin Games community is committed to building technology that enhances our understanding and stewardship of the natural world, responsibly and ethically.

The Australian Agriculture and Trade Bureau? Her eyebrows rose as she read through the details in version 2 again. She went back and clicked on the branch GH_KH. Kangaroo detection, crop protection, audio scare tactics, drone integration. The branch seemed to be using Stella's system to track and deter field pests from above. "Clever, clever, clever," she thought. It was impressive. And it gave her an idea.

With a spark of excitement, she bounded up the stairs, heading straight to her son's room. She knew where the drone she'd given him for Christmas lay, dusty and untouched on a shelf. He'd barely looked at it after unwrapping the shiny box, his mind much more tuned to sports than electronics. A strange twist, given his mother's career as a former chief architect at a top network provider, but she hadn't pushed him.

Back downstairs, Alice held the drone, recalling last year's empty patches in her cornfield and the raucous calls of the crows mocking her. She'd tried everything to keep them away, to no avail. Why not give this a shot? If kangaroo detection could be adapted to scare off crows, then maybe she could reclaim her field.

With a determined smile, she sat down at the table, her mind already racing with modifications. It was time to put her skills to work.

Alice's fingers flew over the keyboard, forking the *GH-KH* branch and spinning up a new instance in her local environment. She adjusted the detection model, tuning it specifically to recognize the size and silhouette of crows in flight. LBBs the birdwatchers called them. She'd dug up a niche dataset from a bird-watching forum, filled with images of crows in various poses, and fed it into the algorithm.

Next, Alice tackled the drone APIs, the "instructions" that allowed different parts of her software to talk to the hardware inside the drone. Since she wasn't working with the exact drone model originally programmed in the project, Alice had to tweak the API to suit her hardware. This was no small task. She was completely unfamiliar with drones and had to figure out exactly how her drone's particular camera, GPS, and other built-in parts could understand the commands in the software.

Once the drone's systems were responding properly, Alice wrote a small script to activate the drone's built-in speaker. With just a few extra lines of code, she hooked it into her audio system, ready to play whatever sounds she deemed fit.

Alice pondered her options, scrolling through a list of sound files she'd collected over the years. She paused as a particularly brilliant idea hit her: what if, instead of a simple air horn, she blasted something iconic? Something unmistakably loud and fierce? She could already picture the crows' feathers ruffling in surprise.

She queued up her choice: the piercing, electrifying scream of Axl Rose from the opening of *Welcome to the Jungle*. A classic, raw, powerful yell, pure rock energy, made to startle. The kind of sound that would jolt even the most fearless crow off its perch.

Alice let out a laugh, imagining the scene: the crows scattering in a panic as Axl's voice tore through the fields. It felt fitting. She'd grown up on '90s rock, and if she was going to fight off pests, she might as well do it with style. She set it up in the system, grinning as she saved the file under a new name: *Crow Buster*.

As she tested it through the drone's speakers, the scream filled the empty kitchen. She nodded, satisfied. "Take that, you feathered fiends," she chuckled. This would be her rock-and-roll defense. Subtle? Not at all. But, after watching crows descend on her corn day after day, Alice had lost all patience. If a few blasts of sound were what it took to protect her crops, then subtlety could go out the window.

The lines of code began stacking up, each one falling into place with a rhythm that felt surprisingly like coming home. She tweaked parameters, adjusted audio thresholds, and ironed out the kinks with a precision she hadn't tapped into since leaving the tech world behind. As the sun dipped below the horizon outside, Alice sat back and looked at her screen. She had built a new kind of scarecrow—one that could take flight and meet her winged opponents on their own turf.

Farming was supposed to be about getting out of high tech. But maybe, just maybe, this blend of old and new could give her a real chance against the crows. And if it didn't? Well, at least she was having fun.

Chapter 11

Alice clicked "Compile" on her laptop, and the quiet kitchen filled with the hum of her computer's fan as her code came to life. Beside her on the table, the small drone sat poised, its propellers glinting in the late afternoon sun. She had spent most of the week tweaking her program, transforming the drone from a simple flying device into a high-tech crow deterrent. Now, instead of just hovering above her fields, the drone would send live, high-resolution images back to her laptop, which would analyze them in real time. As soon as the laptop detected a crow, it would send a command back to the drone, telling it to fly toward the bird and emit a sharp screaming sound to scare it away.

She carried the drone outside, setting it gently on the porch, its tiny camera pointed toward the battered cornfield. The air was still, and a few crows perched on the fence, watching her with unblinking eyes. She launched the drone from her laptop and, with a soft hum, the drone rose into the sky, hovering above the brown stalks like a miniature mechanical guardian. It zipped and spun, flying between rows of corn and capturing live footage of the field below.

On her laptop, her database began filling with new entries as the system detected movement: a line of code for each sighting, each analysis. Data piled up like the notes of a carefully composed symphony, marking the start of her battle against the crows.

ID	Species	First Detected	LatLong	Name
01	*Corvus brachyrhynchos*	01/19/2027 14:11:23.872	41.599998, -72.699997	Chidi Cawley
02	*Sialia sialis*	01/19/2027 14:12:01.013	41.599998, -72.699997	Elenor Azure
03	*Corvus brachyrhynchos*	01/19/2027 14:14:45.998	41.599998, -72.699997	Michael Poe
04	*Macropus fuliginosus*	01/19/2027 14:16:22.514	41.599998, -72.699997	John Jackson

First entry: *Corvus brachyrhynchos*, the American crow.

"Hah!" Alice let out a triumphant laugh, doing a small, victorious dance in her kitchen.

On the second entry, *Sialia sialis*, she furrowed her brow, then quickly looked it up to confirm. It was the Eastern Bluebird. Harmless, she thought, just a little passerby. She added a line to her code to ignore any sightings of Sialia sialis. Her focus, after all, was on the real enemy: the crows. Her eyes narrowed as she watched them flitting across the field, their dark wings slicing through the air.

But the last entry made her pause. *Macropus fuliginosus*—the western gray kangaroo? Confused, she scrolled through the footage. The grainy black-and-white image revealed nothing more than her husband strolling into the field, bending down to adjust the irrigation lines. A laugh escaped her. He'd hate knowing the system had labeled him as an Australian marsupial.

The image recognition software clearly needed some refining; it wasn't exactly trained to distinguish human silhouettes from wildlife. Yet. She made a mental note to add a filter for any more "kangaroo" sightings and excluded them from triggering the drone response. Satisfied, she flew the drone back to the porch and headed inside, her mind already buzzing with ideas for the next round of updates.

Alice's son, Oliver, bounded into the house, sneakers thudding on the wooden floors as he dumped his backpack in the hallway and made a beeline for the fridge. Hearing the familiar clamor, Alice guided the drone back to its perch on the porch, closing her laptop just as Oliver pulled a juice box and an apple from the fridge.

"Hey, kiddo. How was your day?" she asked, giving his hair a gentle ruffle as she passed by. He flashed her a lopsided grin, then managed to squirt juice down his shirt while jabbing the straw into the tiny silver hole in the box.

They settled into their after-school snack routine, chatting about his day as he munched away, and all the while, Alice's gaze drifted to the drone sitting quietly outside. It had worked, in a way. But the reality was she couldn't sit by the screen every day, piloting it manually and keeping watch. She'd need to set it up to patrol the fields on its own—a system with a flight path, something that would circle the crops, scan for movement, and buzz those damn crows whenever they dared to land.

She glanced out the window at the struggling cornfield one last time, her mind already churning through the next steps for automating her "flying scarecrow." The chewed-down stalks might have beaten her for now, but she was ready to fight back. After all, she'd handled tougher challenges like cranky servers, impossible deadlines, and Silicon Valley engineers with far more ambition than actual know-how. Surely, a few crows didn't stand a chance.

Alice reviewed the results from her latest test run. The drone's automated flight path had managed to cover about 95% of her field, but it took a full 75 minutes to complete the sweep. The data was promising, though: the system had identified around 65 creatures in that single pass, including 20 persistent crows and only two kangaroos today. She couldn't help but smile at the names the system had assigned to them, "Steve Irwin" and "Nicole Kidman." The names made her wonder if the language model was matching names to species by nationality. She added that to her growing list of questions for Stella when she ran into her in the fields.

She leaned back, considering how to speed up the drone's rounds. The camera's resolution was good enough that flying the drone a bit higher might still give her the clarity she needed, but cover the area much faster. After some quick calculations, she realized that raising the altitude by 10 feet would be equivalent to zooming out on the camera. This would bring the entire sweep down to under 20 minutes.

As she programmed the update and watched the drone lift off into its adjusted flight path, Alice reached out to @garrett_bauer, the developer who'd built the original branch. She tapped out a quick message.

@alice_chen: I'm testing adjustments to the flight path and altitude to cover my fields faster, but I could use some advice. Anything you'd suggest for improving coverage or detection? Are you experimenting with similar adjustments? Let me know what's been working for you!

Not even a minute later, GitHub pinged with Garrett's enthusiastic response. Alice was curious about the time difference and wondered if he slept.

@garrett_bauer: Raising the altitude def helps. I've been running tests with altitude and field width to boost coverage, but there's still a limit to image quality and line of sight. Use satellite scans for broad overviews and then narrow down with the drone for details.

Intrigued, Alice shot back another message.

@alice_chen: Which satellite platform are you using?

@garrett_bauer: Google Earth Engine. I'll upload the code - still in process but good enough to pull and process field data.

Alice's mind buzzed with possibilities. With a combination of satellite scans and drone details, she'd be able to monitor her fields in real time. She couldn't wait to try Garrett's code.

Alice set up an automatic merge. This would ensure that every line of code that Garrett added would be added to her code as well. She didn't want to miss any of Garrett's updates.

One of the things she learned working in technology is that you let the experts do what they're experts at. She was certain she was not an expert in drones. She was also certain that the

Australian Agriculture and Trade Bureau had far more resources than she did. And, she thought, we're very unlikely to do anything that would be dangerous or cause a security breach.

"Work smarter, not harder," Alice hummed to herself.

Chapter 12

The past weeks had marked a shift for Garrett and Martin. What started as a reluctant partnership—Martin stuck with a bored intern, and Garrett unimpressed by his limited assignments—had slowly transformed. Garrett's enthusiasm for the project had been infectious. Once Martin realized that the kid was onto something useful, something beyond the mundane data-crunching they were assigned, he found himself enjoying the work. Garrett was sharp, eager, and driven by the same kind of curiosity Martin remembered from his early career. Watching Garrett light up as he refined the code, determined to make the drone system come alive, reminded Martin of why he'd entered the field in the first place. The project had taken on a life of its own, transforming their routine workdays into something interesting, even exciting.

Now, they stood in the blazing Australian sun, watching their hard work in motion. Garrett adjusted his sunglasses, squinting as the drone zipped over the vast field, its camera streaming live footage back to their tablets. Dry grass and scrub dotted with trees spread in all directions, while the hum of the drone filled the air. Their code had a singular mission today: deter any kangaroos that dared set foot into their test zone.

"We're live," Garrett whispered to himself while tapping his screen. A small hum filled the air as the drone lifted off. The drone hovered in place, awaiting the next set of commands. Using the satellite data he'd integrated earlier, Martin pulled up a live overlay on his tablet, scanning for any signs of disruption in the field. The satellite images, refreshed every few minutes, showed subtle movements and patterns, grazing trails, flattened grass, and animal pathways. Martin zoomed in on a heat signature near the edge of the field and marked the location.

He'd spotted the critters just as the code highlighted the three figures near the boundary line, their small forms clear against the surrounding scrub. The drone adjusted its flight path, veering toward the suspected intruders with pinpoint accuracy.

"Three kangaroos on the perimeter," Martin announced, tapping the screen to highlight them.

Garrett's stomach did a flip with excitement. This was it. Their code was running out here in the middle of nowhere, finally ready to give these kangaroos a proper scare.

Adjusting its course to approach the nearest kangaroo, the drone hovered 20 feet above the ground, inching closer until it was in range. With a satisfying beep, Garrett's code activated the air horn. A loud, blaring noise cut through the quiet, reverberating across the field.

But the kangaroo didn't even twitch. It stood there, oblivious to the sound, snacking on the grass, barely glancing in the drone's direction.

"Great. Either he's deaf or couldn't care less," Garrett grumbled, glancing at Martin. "We need to tighten up the distance."

He set the drone to swoop in a bit closer on its next pass.

"Two feet," Garrett said, uploading the update. "That should get its attention. Run it again?"

Martin nodded, more than happy to give it another go. The drone circled back, the modified distance set for closer proximity. This time, the air horn blared just a few feet away from the kangaroo, catching it off guard. It startled, held its nose high listening in a tense pause, then bolted, bounding away from the field while kicking up dirt in its wake.

"Now we're getting somewhere," Martin said with a satisfied nod, the edges of a smile forming. But their success was short-lived. On the screen, they noticed another kangaroo, a big one, watching the drone with a mix of indifference and mild curiosity, completely undeterred by the noise. The drone moved closer, air horn blaring in short, repeated blasts, but the kangaroo simply blinked, unmoved. After a few seconds, the drone gave up, hovering briefly before retreating to resume its scan.

"Looks like we've got ourselves a repeat offender," Garrett said, watching the screen as the drone circled back, having failed to shift the kangaroo an inch. "It's just...not enough pressure on the persistent ones."

Martin rubbed his chin, deep in thought. "How about we swarm it? Set up a 'chase protocol' that keeps going until it's clear out of the field?"

Garrett's eyes lit up. "A swarming protocol! Yes! We program it so the drone pursues the kangaroo aggressively, hovers close, and continues blasting the horn, but without making physical contact. Get it to the edge of the field and stop there."

"Only target repeat offenders," Martin added, getting into the idea. "A single scare pass for first-timers, but if they come back, they're in for a chase."

"Exactly. We'll set it to stop once they're out of crop range," Garrett agreed, already scrolling through the code to make adjustments. "Drone backs off once the kangaroo's past the boundary."

He worked quickly, tapping away as the heat bore down on them, modifying the drone's behavior to make it more relentless, more insistent on driving the kangaroo out of the protected zone. He programmed in the swarming protocol, adding a buffer to ensure the drone didn't cross the field boundaries, but instead followed the intruder right to the edge, giving it no choice but to leave.

"All right, let's see if they like *this*," Garrett said, pushing the final code update.

They sent the drone out again, holding their breath as the drone zeroed in on the third kangaroo, their designated "repeat offender." As the drone neared, the air horn blared, and this time, instead of retreating, the drone followed at a close distance, circling the animal and nudging it closer to the edge. The kangaroo hesitated, as if it might stand its ground. But the relentless buzzing and noise from the air horn convinced it to turn and bound away, the drone following it until it was safely out of the field.

"Heh," Martin said, with a grin he rarely allowed himself. "Now *that's* how you handle a persistent one."

Garrett laughed, exhilarated. "Do they give out awards in agriculture? Because I think we're on to something here."

They watched as the drone returned to its scanning position, slowly flying back and forth protectively over the field, ready for the next pest. The flight path wasn't perfect, but it was close. And as far as Garrett was concerned, they were just getting started.

Chapter 13

Stella was used to sharing the field path with birdwatchers, their binoculars trained on the woods in hopes of glimpsing the elusive Connecticut warbler. When the small, yellow-bellied bird flitted across their sights, it often drew reverent gasps. But today, with the snow blanketing the trail, there were no warblers, no gasps, no camouflaged enthusiasts tucked into the brush. It was just Stella and Finnick trampling through the snow-covered fields.

The isolation took her back to the pandemic days when people stayed hidden in their homes and her walks grew quiet, her world reduced to this trail and her loyal companion. Through those long, lonely months, Finnick had been her steady sanity; an anchor to the ordinary. As they made their way along the field today, the only sounds were the crunch of snow and a strange buzzing, faint but persistent. Not bees; it was much too early for them to emerge. The noise was higher-pitched, almost like a whine.

Then she saw it. A small craft hovering just above the cornstalks, barely visible through the faint morning light.

"A drone," Stella thought.

The drone swept toward the edge of the field, pausing just a few feet ahead of them before it turned back moving in smooth calculated sweeps. Stella nudged Finnick forward, her mind circling back to her latest idea to use algorithmic models to trace the intricate threads of penguin ancestry.

She wanted to make family trees automatic, to create not just a map of where a penguin was born, but a deep, layered genealogy that stretched back generations. Imagine being able to track an entire line—grandparents, great-grandparents, uncles, cousins—all weaving back to that one specific penguin. It was more than just science; it was a way to show the connection between these animals and the ancient paths their families had carved through the Antarctic.

And then, an idea struck her. What if she let sponsors name the lineages? Not just a one-off penguin, but an entire clan carrying the sponsor's name. Someone could adopt a family, save them from the looming threats of climate and pollution, and know that for as long as the colony survived, there would be a whole line of "Everdeens" waddling across the ice. She smiled, picturing the fields of names like "Smith," "Chen," and "Martinez" attached to generations of penguins. It could be beautiful, a permanent reminder that humans had a role in the lives of these creatures and an obligation to protect them.

Stella could already see the stories writing themselves: the Smiths migrating across glaciers, the Chens nesting by the frozen shoreline, and maybe, just maybe, a sprawling Everdeen clan.

It wasn't long before a familiar figure appeared up ahead, bundled in a thick green parka, hands shoved deep into her pockets. Alice, her breath swirling like smoke in the cold morning air, was trudging through the snow, eyes on the horizon.

Stella raised a gloved hand in greeting as they closed the distance. "Hey, Alice! Is that your son's drone?"

Alice chuckled, glancing over the field where brittle cornstalks poked through the snow. "Not anymore. It's mine now."

Stella slowed her pace, letting her steps fall into sync with Alice's as they walked the trails on the border of the fields, the silence between them feeling warm against the chill. Finnick bounded ahead, nose deep in the snow, occasionally glancing back to make sure they were still following. For a moment, neither spoke as the peacefulness of the early snow wrapped around them. Finally, Alice broke the quiet, her voice casual yet carrying an edge of curiosity.

"I've been meaning to ask you," Alice began, her breath puffing in little clouds. "I saw your latest updates on 'The Penguin Games' repository. Quite the setup you've got there. Are you going to Antarctica to test it out?"

Stella glanced sideways, catching the glint of a smile at the corner of Alice's lips. The question hung between them, light yet brimming with something else, as if Alice were testing the waters, daring her to share more. Stella felt a grin tugging at her mouth as she looked toward the horizon, imagining the vast icy landscape, dotted not with trees and snow-covered fields but with endless stretches of white and the tiny figures of penguins in the distance.

"It's not exactly a quick trip," she said, a touch of wistfulness in her voice. "But I'd love to see it in action in its natural habitat, not just running on my monitors." She hesitated, then added, "But Finnick... It's too long a time to leave him alone."

Alice nodded thoughtfully, glancing ahead as Finnick darted through the snow. "Well," she said, as if it were the most obvious thing in the world, "I could watch him. You know he loves these fields. Already acts like he owns the place." She laughed, the sound warm in the cold air. "Seriously, though. What you're doing is incredible. If going to Antarctica lets you see it come to life, you should do it."

Stella paused, looking at Alice, her face open and sincere in the cold light of morning. It wasn't often that someone in her life encouraged her to go further, to risk more for the sake of her work. For a long time, she'd felt like an outsider in her field, running her race in silence, rarely stopping to enjoy the view. But Alice.... Alice had stepped right in, seeing not only the code but the meaning behind it.

"Thank you," Stella said, her voice a bit softer. "Sometimes, I wonder if it's all worth it, you know? This work, the late nights, the thousands of lines of code. But you get it."

Alice's eyes sparkled, a hint of a conspiratorial grin playing on her lips. "I get it."

"I've been using your software." Alice pointed across the field to where the drone was hovering, bobbing in the breeze like a watchful eye. "Made a few tweaks, you could say."

Stella's eyebrows shot up, her curiosity piqued. "Oh? 'Tweaks,' you say? Do tell."

Alice chuckled, slowing their pace further. "Well, I may have borrowed your identification framework. Just a few adjustments for...crows, mostly." Her voice dropped, almost sheepish. "You'd be amazed at how useful your setup is for scaring them off."

Stella laughed, delighted. "A penguin-tracking system turned kangaroo hunter turned crow deterrent. I never thought I'd see the day." She shook her head, a look of admiration slipping into her gaze.

Alice's grin widened, and she tilted her head toward the field behind them. "It keeps finding kangaroos."

Stella couldn't help but laugh, the sound carrying across the empty field.

Alice smiled and reminded Stella of something she'd nearly forgotten: the joy of creation, not just in solitude but in connection, knowing her work could have a life of its own beyond her. They walked on, trading ideas and thoughts, their words flowing freely, the drone a quiet guardian humming quietly above, sharing the snowy fields with them.

"No, really, it keeps finding kangaroos," Alice said. "The LLM named them Steve Irwin and Nicole Kidman."

Stella tilted her head, processing the oddity. "It must be from the GH-KH branch. We tuned the image identification to favor kangaroo markers."

Alice's lips twitched as she stared at the snow-dusted trail ahead. "That makes sense. But if misidentifications are this common, it's only a matter of time before it calls my husband a wombat."

The corners of Stella's mouth twitched. Alice didn't just drop casual observations—she was working through something. The pause in her step was as telling as a lightbulb flickering on.

"What if the issue is the algorithm's bias and the way the data is gathered?" Alice said, her voice gaining momentum. "I've been thinking about how to expand the drone's camera range without sacrificing resolution. It would capture more detail, faster. If it works, you wouldn't just solve the crow-versus-kangaroo problem; it could make your Antarctica trip a whole lot more efficient."

Stella slowed, her full attention now locked on Alice. "I'm all ears. I've been working on a module for lineage detection—tracking penguin families through visual markers. If we nail that, it could reshape how researchers map colonies."

The air between them hummed with possibility, their strides falling into a rhythm as ideas unfolded like a blueprint written in snow. For a moment, the trail ahead felt less like an ordinary path and more like the start of something bigger.

They stopped at the edge of the field, inspired by their conversation and in awe of the beauty surrounding them as the last rays of sunlight stretched across the snowy landscape, casting a warm, golden glow over everything. Stella could see in Alice's face that thrill of collaborative problem-solving that she knew all too well. It was something shared, a language that didn't need words.

"Well, don't keep it to yourself," Stella said, her smile widening. "Let's hear it."

Alice's hands flew into motion, gesturing as she outlined her idea, her voice animated as she explained the adjustments she had in mind. Finnick, oblivious to the weight of the conversation, rolled blissfully in the snow at their feet, his fur gathering white flakes that sparkled in the fading light. The quiet field around them felt alive with possibility, the air humming not just with the faint sound of the drone, but with the ideas that danced between them. Each fed off the other, a small spark growing into something bigger.

For a moment, Stella felt a sense of clarity, a shared excitement that brought the future into sharp focus. This was why she'd put her work out there, for connections like this. And as Alice spoke, it felt like the beginning of something important: A friendship bound not just by proximity, but by the things they could build together.

Chapter 14

Martin cleared his throat, tapping the laptop screen to bring up the first slide as the small team of Agriculture and Trade Bureau executives settled into the conference room. Garrett sat beside him, wearing his one button-down shirt, hands clasped tightly, a mixture of excitement and nerves flashing across his face.

"Let's get started," Martin said, scanning the room. "As you know, Garrett and I have been testing a new approach to protect crops from the kangaroos damaging crop fields. He's successfully integrated drone technology to deter the kangaroos, and I think you'll like what he's come up with."

Martin clicked on a video clip, and the room went dark as the screen filled with aerial footage. A field spread out below, with rows of crops and a trio of kangaroos off to one side. A small drone buzzes into the scene, moving in calculated arcs, keeping pace with one of the kangaroos before letting out a loud, blaring noise. The animal hesitated, ears twitching before it bounded away, retreating toward the field's edge.

One of the executives, arms crossed, leaned forward with interest. "That's impressive," he murmured, as the clip played on, showing more footage of the drone's maneuvers scaring off kangaroos one by one.

Martin nodded, suppressing a smile. "So far, it's working as expected. Garrick has programmed a 'chase' mode for repeat offenders, so the drone won't give up until they've cleared the field perimeter."

The video faded, and Martin clicked to a slide that highlighted the project's positives.

Garrett chimed in, "This system could significantly reduce the damage kangaroos are causing to crops. Our test runs have shown that the drones can cover a lot of ground in a short time. We're getting close to ninety-five percent field coverage."

"And with minimal human intervention," Martin added. "The drones run autonomously, only requiring occasional adjustments. They free up manpower and let us apply targeted deterrence without fences or additional barriers."

"This is promising," Martin's manager said.

Martin flipped to the next slide. "We're thrilled about the results. In our first donzen trial runs, one out of three kangaroos leave the vicinity of a field on the first warning airhorn blast. The remaining kangaroos leave the area within three passes."

Garrett chimed in, "But there are some risks." The executives looked at each other, their expressions shifting slightly.

Garrett took over, his voice steady as he pointed to the screen. "First, there's the possibility of disrupting local wildlife. Kangaroos might be chased off, but other animals could be unintentionally affected as well. If we expand the use of drones, we could alter some local ecosystems."

An executive shifted in his seat. "How can you minimize the impact?"

"We think that we can reduce it with better targeting," Garrett replied, "but there are limits. Drones detect movement, and they can't always identify specific animals. And then there's the matter of... well, physical interference."

Martin jumped in. "There's a risk of injury if a drone collides with an animal or person. And if a kangaroo were to accidentally knock a drone out of the air, we'd be dealing with repair costs and, potentially, the loss of a valuable asset. Plus, if a drone crashes due to battery failure or an unexpected error, it becomes litter."

"We tried to adjust flight altitude, but that reduced deterrence," Garrett added. "And it shortens battery life, which brings me to another issue: limited operational hours."

A manager scribbled a note, glancing up with an arched eyebrow. "What are you seeing on battery life?"

Garrett looked to Martin, who answered, "Around two hours forty minutes per charge. We're working on it, but right now it's limiting. It means we need a recharge system in the field if we want continuous coverage."

The executives exchanged glances, nodding thoughtfully.

Garrett cleared his throat. "And there's also the potential for privacy issues. Drones capturing footage over farmland might inadvertently record people. We may record farm workers, landowners, and anyone who happens to be in the fields. We'd need strict data protocols to prevent misuse of that footage."

"Is there a way to block those recordings?" another executive asked.

"Possibly," Martin said.

Garrett flipped to the final point on the slide. "The drones are connected to the Agriculture and Trade Bureau's main network. This is the government network that holds our research and personnel data. If someone hacks into them, they could turn the drones against us, use them to damage crops, or even collect sensitive data. We need more security expertise if we're going to roll this out on a larger scale."

The room grew quiet as the team considered the implications. Finally, one of the senior managers spoke up.

"I appreciate the thoroughness, both of you," he said, folding his hands on the table. "This is important work, and while the risks are clear, the potential is even clearer. Here's what I'm proposing. We'll authorize short-term funding and deployment of five existing drones. But I want a tabletop security exercise conducted. Simulate scenarios where the system could be compromised, and I want a team to evaluate responses and vulnerabilities. And we want a live demo in two weeks."

Martin and Garrett nodded, the weight of responsibility settling between them.

"I'll make the arrangements," Martin said.

The executives rose from their seats, nodding their approval as they filed out. Martin turned to Garrett, a rare smile breaking across his face. "Looks like we're funded, kid."

Garrett grinned back while shaking his head, excited, but not entirely sure of what he had gotten himself into. Two weeks until a live demo? At least the project would look good on his resume.

Chapter 15

Alice sat at her farmhouse table looking at the latest updates from GH-KH. Garrett and his team had added an intriguing feature—an improved "repeat offender" protocol, designed to chase off stubborn animals that kept coming back. She smiled to herself, picturing the drone darting over the cornfield, a mechanical screaming scarecrow with a vendetta against persistent pests. She closed the updates, glancing out the window to where the drone sat on the porch, ready for its next round of crow deterrence.

As the program loaded, she heard the familiar creak of boots on the floor behind her. Her husband, Paul, walked in from the fields, brushing the dust from his hands, his dark hair covered in a layer of dirt, his face weathered and warm. His gaze landed on her screen, where lines of code flickered under her fingers, and he grinned.

"Looks like you're back in tech mode," he said, as he leaned over her shoulder with his eyebrows raised in amused admiration.

Alice looked up at him, smiling. "I think I am. And this time, it's for a good cause. Keeping the crows out of our crops."

Paul chuckled, crossing his arms as he watched her work. "Well, from what I've seen, that little drone's doing a good job so far. Those crows have been staying out of sight more often than not."

She gave a mock sigh of relief. "Finally, something listens to me around here."

Paul laughed, pulling a chair up beside her and sitting down with an affectionate look in his eyes. They had worked side by side since they bought the farm, each bringing their expertise to the table. She had poured her knowledge of systems and problem-solving into every field row and irrigation line, and he had brought his patience, strength, and know-how of the land. Together, they had built something meaningful, even if it was still rough around the edges.

"You know," Alice said, leaning into him, "I was thinking…if this works, really works, we could make it something bigger. Not just for us, but for other farmers, too. Imagine it, a software business where we help other small farms keep their crops safe."

Paul raised his eyebrows, a spark of pride in his eyes. "I always knew you'd get back to building something. I love the idea. So, what do you need?"

She looked at him, eyes shining. "A few more drones. I want to run more test sweeps and get more coverage. I think if I could show it works in our fields, other farms might be interested. Plus, the new updates could let us target different areas, even coordinate with other types of equipment." She paused, her excitement spilling over as she gestured to her laptop. "The open source is good. And this code I built on top of it, Paul, it's brilliant. I think it could be the start of something amazing."

Paul reached over, taking her hand in his. "Go for it. If you believe in this, I'm behind you all the way."

She felt a warmth spread through her, a reminder of why she had married him. He'd never once held her back, not when she'd decided to leave her stable job, not when she insisted they buy the land and take a chance. For him, her ambition was part of who she was, and he wouldn't have it any other way.

With renewed determination, Alice pulled up the specs for the new drone, already envisioning the new flight paths she could map out and the potential for automated sweeps and targeted flights. Together, they discussed the logistics, debating which fields needed the most protection and how they could test out different deterrence methods.

The future seemed to spread out before her, fields full of possibilities. She knew they'd tackle it together, every line of code and every stubborn crow along the way.

Chapter 16

Alice stood at the edge of the muddy field, watching her drones zip back and forth over the newly planted corn, their cameras glinting in the midday sun. With three drones patrolling, she felt a sense of pride, a certain satisfaction in the fruits of her labor. They moved autonomously now, a testament to the countless hours she'd poured into the code. With each sweep, they sent back images and data, feeding her model, identifying intruders, and keeping an eye out for pests. For the first time in a long time, she felt she had control over her small slice of land.

Yet, beneath the excitement, a sliver of unease flickered. Alice watched as one drone veered off its programmed path, angling sharply toward a patch of tall grass. She tapped her laptop, checking the signal to see if some wildlife was in its sights, but nothing appeared. The screen just showed a streak of pixelated green, with no sign of movement. "Weird," she thought, tapping at the controls to bring the drone back to the grid.

As if in response, the second drone swung around, adjusting its altitude, its camera tilting with purpose like it had picked up something she couldn't see. Her fingers stilled on the keyboard. That wasn't part of the program.

She shook her head, chalking it up to a minor glitch. After all, every new system had its kinks. She'd debug it later.

Just as she was about to pull her attention back to her screen, Paul came striding across the field, waving at her with one hand, the other clutching a wrench. "Alice!" he called, his voice faint in the open air. She could tell by his stride that he was in good spirits, and she grinned, lifting her hand in a quick wave.

The smile faded as she caught movement in her peripheral vision. One of the drones was altering course, edging toward Paul. She squinted at the screen, feeling her pulse quicken as the drone tilted forward, its camera now fully trained on him. Her fingers flew over the keyboard as she punched in a command to reroute it. But the drone ignored her, continuing its glide toward Paul, accelerating in fits and starts.

"Paul!" she shouted, her voice tight with urgency. He stopped mid-stride, looking back at her, a puzzled expression on his face. "Hold still!"

Paul looked up, finally spotting the drone as it buzzed dangerously close to his head. "What the—?" His eyes widened as he ducked, narrowly missing the metal body as it whizzed past his shoulder, circling him like a hawk sizing up its prey.

Alice's heart hammered in her chest. She tapped frantically at the keyboard, trying to override the command. "Come on, come on…. " Her screen flashed, the drone finally pulling away and returning back to its original path. She exhaled, her shoulders slumping as she watched it return to the field.

Paul walked over, his face a mix of amusement and irritation. "You almost got me there," he said, attempting a smile but shaken.

Alice shook her head, the moment's adrenaline making her hands tremble. "It wasn't supposed to do that. It's got specific flight paths."

Paul shrugged, his usual calm demeanor intact, though his eyes held a hint of caution. "Hey, I know you know what you're doing. But these things…maybe they're starting to think a little too much for themselves?"

She attempted a laugh, though it came out hollow. "Maybe they're just getting too ambitious."

But her gaze drifted back to the screen, where the drones hovered dutifully, seemingly harmless, going about their rounds. That gnawing feeling returned. The technology was pushing boundaries, but this…this was something different.

Even as they shared a moment of quiet, Alice couldn't shake the feeling that her drones, her creation, were evolving in ways she hadn't anticipated. There was a line somewhere between progress and control, and for the first time, she wondered if she might be crossing it.

Chapter 17

Martin squinted against the harsh Australian sun, feeling sweat gather at the back of his neck as he scanned the field, his eyes following the drones as they zipped back and forth. There were too many eyes on this for his taste. As someone who had gone many years avoiding all eyes, he fought off a panic attack. The Australian Agriculture and Trade Bureau executives stood in a tight huddle behind him, watching each drone movement with a hawkish intensity. To them, this was an investment, a trial of funding, resources, and promises. To Martin, this was his chance, the closest he'd been to real success in years.

"Looks like it's holding steady," he observed, mostly to himself, though Garrett caught it from a few feet away.

Garrett's response was quick and eager, "Smooth as butter." The kid sounded confident, but Martin recognized that jittery edge, the nervousness just barely hidden under a layer of bravado. This trial felt different, heavier. With every line of code, every pixel on the live feed, Martin sensed the pressure building. He could feel it in the furrowed brows and crossed arms of the observers behind him, ready to pounce at the slightest misstep.

The drones were sweeping the fields in clean, even lines, and for a moment, Martin allowed himself to feel pride. With the soft hum of the drones mixed with the rustling of dry leaves, he felt the unusual blend of tech and nature settle over him in a rare, calming way. Maybe, just maybe, they were going to pull this off.

One of the drones wobbled, dipping suddenly and swerving off its path. Martin's stomach twisted as Garrett, eyes wide, waited to see what would happen. A repeat visitor. The drone approached the first time, blaring the airhorn just as expected. When the kangaroo didn't move, the drone swooped around and approached a second time, getting even closer. The drone continued to pursue the stubborn animal. The drone backed up and then gained speed, horn blaring, headed straight for a large gray figure grazing by the field's edge.

"Ah, no," Garrett hissed, his fingers darting over the screen. The drone picked up speed, too fast now, and then—thud. The machine smacked into the kangaroo's side, bouncing off and skidding to a halt in a dusty, graceless heap. Seemingly unhurt, the kangaroo shook its head and bounded off, but Martin could feel the weight of eyes on his back, every head in the huddle turning to him with the unspoken question: "What went wrong?"

Martin forced himself to stay calm, clearing his throat, but his mouth was dry. He looked over at Garrett, trying to keep his expression steady, but Garrett looked as rattled as he felt. Martin's jaw tightened, and he threw Garrett a look of frustration mixed with resignation. "So much for smooth," he sighed, stepping back as the officials closed in, their murmurs growing louder, faces tight with concern.

One of the department heads, a tall man with a hard gaze, cut through the murmurs. "We'll need to address this," he said, looking directly at Martin and Garrett. His tone was calm but laced with an unmistakable firmness. "This can't happen again. Understand?"

Garrett shifted uncomfortably, irritation flickering in his eyes. "It was an anomaly," he said, trying to sound steady. "The drones are still in testing. This is just one incident."

The official didn't blink. "One incident could mean bad headlines."

Martin felt his stomach drop. This was supposed to be his moment, his project to own, and now it was at risk over one mistake. He forced himself to sound calm as he addressed the group. "We'll look into it straight away," he said, willing confidence into his voice. "We'll go through the logs, figure out what caused the error, and make sure it doesn't happen again."

The official nodded, but his gaze was hard as steel. "See that you do," he said, and his eyes flicked to

Garrett. "Or we'll be forced to shut this project down."

As the officials turned away, heading back to their vehicles, Garrett let out a low, frustrated laugh. "It's a test. Of course, things will go wrong," he whispered defensively, his voice cracking from nerves.

Martin shot him a sharp look. The kid didn't understand how things worked here, not really. "We need to figure out what went wrong and fix it," he said, his voice firm.

Garrett's irritation turned into something darker: anxiety. "Martin, a drone just rammed into a kangaroo. I didn't program it to do that. It was supposed to keep a safe distance, but it veered right into the poor animal."

The more Garrett spoke, the more his nerves unraveled, and Martin could see it happening. The kid was realizing he might be in over his head. Martin sighed, rubbing his temples. "Look, I don't like it either. It shouldn't have happened, but we can't let one glitch ruin this."

Garrett's face was clouded with doubt. "But how am I supposed to fix this if I don't even know what went wrong?"

Martin felt a pang of empathy but didn't have time for Garrett's doubts. Not now. Not when his career was finally getting somewhere. "Listen," he said, keeping his voice steady. "This isn't just about the tech. There's a bigger picture here. Funding. If we lose their backing, this whole project goes down the drain."

Garrett sighed, the fight draining from his face. "I don't know what happened. I'm programming alone. This kind of project needs structured testing, more eyes. Probably some experts. I can't do this alone."

"You're not alone," Martin said firmly. "We'll get into the code, figure out what's mucked up, and sort it. But we're not broadcasting every little stumble."

Martin watched Garrett's expression tighten at the word "we." He knew what the kid was thinking: Martin didn't write code. He could barely read it, let alone contribute. But that wasn't the point, and it didn't matter. Garrett didn't see it yet, but they were a team. Martin wasn't going to leave him to drown in this alone.

The flicker of doubt on Garrett's face softened, shifting into reluctant understanding. He didn't have to like it, Martin thought. He just had to get it. Stepping closer, Martin clapped a hand on Garrett's shoulder. His voice carried a surprising warmth even to his own ears. "Come on. Let's get back to the drawing board. We'll make it better. We'll make it work."

As they headed back to their makeshift command post, Martin felt the weight settle over his shoulders. This wasn't just about Garrett or the code—it was about him too. With just weeks to make the project bulletproof, Martin felt a deep resolve. He wasn't going to let this slip through his fingers. This was his chance to step up, to prove he wasn't just another mid-level manager coasting through his career. He was all in now.

Chapter 18

Violet stared at her screen, eyes narrowed, a cup of lukewarm tea forgotten beside her. She'd been sifting through the code repositories for hours now, hopping between more than 50 new the-penguin-games branches, her brow creasing deeper with each discovery. She'd expected the forks to veer off in slightly different directions—after all, that was the beauty of open source. But this? It was a lot. One security firm out of Rhode Island was making an app to chase the geese off of their rich clients' lawns. Someone up in Montana was naming buffalo. Even Garrett's and Alice's branches were moving faster than she'd anticipated, the forks pulsing with new algorithms and unfamiliar subroutines she hadn't seen before.

Scrolling through Garrett's project, GH-KH, Violet spotted a new layer of code labeled innocuously as "Object Avoidance Protocol 2." But as she dug in, her suspicions flared. This wasn't just any object avoidance code—it was sophisticated, far beyond the standard navigation algorithms for keeping drones from colliding with trees or fences. Violet's fingers hovered over the trackpad, her pulse quickening. Garrett had somehow worked in algorithms that could maneuver drones dynamically, shifting altitude and trajectory in real-time as if anticipating obstacles before they even entered the drone's path.

"Steering and maneuvering," she muttered to herself, biting her lip as she read line after line of code. But something felt off. This wasn't purely about avoidance. It seemed almost predatory, the way it tracked and honed in on moving targets with precise adjustments.

Violet's gaze drifted to the time on her screen. Midnight. She couldn't shake the feeling that Garrett's project was slipping beyond her control, veering off into territory she hadn't envisioned. With a resigned sigh, she opened her contacts and sent a quick message to Stella.

Violet: You up? Found something strange in the code. Need a second opinion.

The response came moments later, almost as if Stella had been waiting.

Stella: Always. Call?

In minutes, Stella's face appeared on the screen, her silver curls haloed in the soft light of her home office. She looked calm and composed, a contrast to Violet's edgy demeanor.

"All right, what am I looking at?" Stella asked, adjusting her glasses as Violet shared her screen.

122

Violet took a breath, gesturing to the lines of code she'd highlighted. "This is in Garrett's fork. Look here, Object Avoidance Protocol 2. It's not standard. I think he's borrowed from automotive AI algorithms that are typically used for self-driving cars to maneuver around obstacles."

Stella leaned in, her eyes scanning the screen, a slight frown forming. "Interesting…. Seems harmless enough. If anything, it's meant to keep the drones safer. Maybe he's just trying to protect the crops without hurting the kangaroos.."

Violet's lips pressed together, a skeptical look crossing her face. "That's what I thought at first. But the way it's written, it doesn't seem like it's just avoiding its target. The patterns here…it almost looks like it's steering toward certain objects, zeroing in on them. I've seen this type of logic in other projects, but it's usually applied for…well, let's just say it's not for harmless wildlife monitoring."

Stella arched an eyebrow, meeting Violet's gaze. "You think he's programmed the drones to chase targets?"

Violet nodded, biting her lip. "I do. I mean, look at these adjustments—if the object moves left, the drone veers to intercept. If the object speeds up, so does the drone. This isn't just avoidance. It's active pursuit."

Stella leaned back, tapping her fingers thoughtfully on the edge of her desk. "Let's play devil's advocate. Maybe Garrett's trying to keep his drones close to the target to deter them more effectively. There's still a distance rule, keeping the drones a meter from any object."

Violet felt a surge of frustration but held it back, choosing her words carefully. "Stella, this doesn't feel like deterrence. It feels like escalation. If he's using car algorithms to maneuver, he's pushing these drones into an active role—no longer just monitoring like our code, but directly engaging. And if these algorithms are off… well, what's stopping one of these drones from mistaking a human for a 'target'?"

Stella sighed, brushing a stray curl from her face. "Look, I see where you're coming from. We can send a note to ask Garrick about it. He probably didn't intend for the code to track and escalate to the degree it's reading to us."

Violet's gaze didn't waver. "Maybe. But it's not just Garrett." She switched tabs, pulling up Alice's fork, scrolling quickly to a section tagged "Repeat Offender Detection 2." "Alice's code here…she's merged in the algorithms to track and respond differently to 'repeat offenders.'"

Stella let out a slow breath, her expression turning serious. "Okay. But let's not raise alarm bells just yet. They're experimenting. We knew that was part of the deal when we made the code open source."

Violet nodded, though the uneasy feeling in her stomach didn't fade. "I just… I don't want to see this tech spiraling into something we can't control. What happens if these 'repeat offenders' aren't just crows or kangaroos?"

Stella gave a reassuring smile. "We'll handle it, Violet. Let's not get ahead of ourselves. But I'll keep my eye on it, too."

The screen dimmed as Stella signed off, but Violet stayed, staring at the lines of code dancing before her. She knew Stella was trying to keep her calm and to reassure her. But as she returned to Garrett's repository and traced through the lines of pursuit logic once more, a chill ran down her spine. The feeling that she was missing something, something big, only grew stronger.

Chapter 19

Stella felt the telltale throb of a migraine setting in as she gazed at the wall of code in front of her with a furrowed brow. Lines of data flickered across her screen, each one more unsettling than the last. Violet's tone last night was unusually urgent. She rarely sounded the alarm, so when she did, it made Stella pause.

Stella trusted Violet's instincts. Her colleague wasn't one to get rattled easily; she handled high-stakes projects with the cool composure of someone who'd spent years deciphering complex data. If she'd flagged this issue, more was at stake than the repercussions of a minor glitch.

Stella pulled up the recent modifications to the GH-KH branch and scrutinized Garrett's updates. At first glance, everything looked sound. The "repeat offender" protocol was a clever addition, designed to discourage animals from repeatedly encroaching on certain areas. But as Stella dug deeper, she felt a cold prickle of dread. The model wasn't just differentiating animals; it was learning to categorize "threats" based on environmental cues, motion patterns, and even past logs. In short, it was deciding what was "hostile" based on incomplete data, and she could already see the troubling implications.

As she dissected the code further, she noticed an algorithm layer labeled "Behavioral Override". Her heart sank as she realized what the AI algorithm was doing. The drones weren't avoiding obstacles; they were targeting specific animals. The algorithms driving the drones were telling them to track specific visual markers, movements, and shapes. The more a particular pattern appeared in the field, the more likely the AI program would tell the drones to mark it as a "repeat offender" and respond with increasing hostility.

She closed her eyes, releasing a slow, controlled breath. The problem was unmistakable: the system could easily mistake any un-excluded mammal, like a person crossing the field multiple times, for a pest. Garrett's approach was risky. He had the LLM set to interpret unknown objects when the image recognition failed to make a definitive match. Under the wrong conditions, the drones might classify that person as a threat and start swarming.

The swarming code had a critical flaw: there was no minimum distance safeguard. What Garrett had implemented was known as a microstep. The code established an initial safe distance of one meter to keep the drones from an animal. But if the animal didn't leave the protected area, the drone would close in by half, reducing the distance to half a meter, then a quarter of a meter, and so on, until it reached a distance approaching zero. What Garrett had overlooked, however, was the point from which the distance was measured. It was being calculated from the center of the drone, not accounting for the drone's propellers, which extended at least six inches on each side. This miscalculation meant that, at some point, collision was inevitable.

Stella's hands trembled as she opened the internal messaging app and typed a response to Violet. "You were right to worry. Garrett's update is making the system too aggressive. And there are no safeguards. It would confuse a person for an intruder if they're in the field and the image is blurry."

Her fingers hesitated over the keyboard as a new thought hit her: Alice. She remembered Alice mentioning the tweaks she'd integrated from GH-KH into her farm drones. Alice had been so thrilled about the updates, eager to make her drones more autonomous and efficient. But with these new findings, Stella's excitement about Alice's project twisted into a knot of fear.

She texted Alice immediately.

Stella: turn off the drones I found a bug

Swallowing her anxiety, she tried calling again, but still nothing. The image of Alice out there, unwittingly facing a swarm of increasingly hostile machines, sent a chill down her spine.

Alice: i let the batteries die last night
  they targeted Paul in the field
yesterday
  figured it was something i did

With a renewed sense of urgency, Stella returned to her laptop, typing furiously. She had to patch this, and fast. She put in a hard stop in the aggression algorithm - no closer than a meter. Ever. A small change but one Garrett had failed to put in. Then she began coding a critical update to block the drones from tracking humans entirely, writing it to override the machine learning protocols that Garrett had introduced. It was a blunt solution, one that would reduce the drones' responsiveness, but she couldn't risk waiting.

Her fingers flew over the keyboard as she crafted a custom filter to force the system to ignore any behavior patterns that could be associated with people - movements, shapes, even clothing colors. She couldn't allow a machine to decide, based on skewed parameters, who or what was a threat.

Stella paused, her gaze resting on a photo of her and Finnick on the edge of her desk. She'd built this project on the belief that technology could help protect the environment, that it could be a force for good. When she was told that by agreeing to work with National Scientific she would have to open source the code, she had known the risks. Once any code is is out of your hands and into the hands of the world, you give up control and it could be used for nefarious purposes. She still believed that the benefits to the penguin project outweighed the risk of bad actors. But wondered if her decision would come back to haunt her.

With a final keystroke, she pushed the code update, setting it to propagate to every fork of the repository. As she watched the system process her changes, she crafted a message for everyone using the software:

"Urgent: All users, please download the latest update immediately. This patch prevents collision and human tracking within the 'repeat offender' model. Ensure your systems are synced. This is a critical safety measure."

Her finger hovered over the send button. She closed her eyes, breathed deeply, and pressed it. The message flashed out, leaving her sitting alone in the quiet of her home, the snoring of the dog filling the silence.

Chapter 20

Garrett sat hunched over his laptop, his fingers hovering uncertainly over the keys as lines of code glared back at him, unyielding and relentless. He'd been staring at this screen for weeks, sifting through algorithm after algorithm, each more complex than the last. No matter how many adjustments he made, there was this gnawing feeling at the pit of his stomach, the fear that he was in over his head.

When Garrett saw Stella Everdeen's message this morning about a safety update for the drone software, he felt a rush of relief wash over him, as if he'd been holding his breath for days and finally exhaled. Stella's update outlined a new protocol: object collision prevention and a human recognition filter that prevented the drones from mistakenly tagging people as repeat offenders. Her message was clear and to the point, with a note about the importance of adopting this change for ongoing safety.

"Hey," Garrett said to Martin over the cubical wall. "Stella Everdeen sent an update. She's added a filter to prevent the drones from hitting animals and tagging people as threats. If we integrate her code, we fix the issue."

Martin kept typing. "If she's set it up, we're in good hands."

Garrett pushed his chair back and rubbed his eyes. The fluorescent lights in the office felt harsher than usual, casting a cold, sterile glow over his cubicle. The tension in his shoulders had crept up into his neck, and his mind buzzed with a thousand questions he didn't have the answers to.

Garrett took a deep breath, swallowing his pride, and walked over to Martin. Martin glanced up, uneasy when he saw Garrett's expression.

"Martin," Garrett's voice was quieter than usual.

"Yeah," Martin swiveled to face him fully, concern flickering in his eyes. Garrett took a breath, steadying himself. "It's this project. I don't...I mean, I'm not sure I'm experienced enough to guarantee the code is safe. There are so many algorithms, and each tweak seems to create new issues. I don't want to mess this up."

Garrett looked down at his hands as Martin studied him for a moment. Martin's gaze softened as he reassured the intern. "Garrett, you're doing a top job. When I was your age, I was playing around with data logs, nothing close to this."

Garrett managed a small smile, but his unease lingered. "I keep thinking that one wrong line of code could make this all go sideways. I'm trying to get the drones to respond accurately, to know when something's a real threat. But it's just…you know, a harmless animal. Kangaroos cause a mess, but they aren't evil. But I…I don't want to leave this place without a good reference. I go back next week. I don't know if I can finish this safely."

For the first time in decades, Martin had a taste of what it felt like to be successful. And he wasn't going to let this kid screw up his chance.

Martin leaned back, folding his arms. "Garrett, it's ok to admit when you're in over your head Better to own up than to stumble through blindly. The tech we're dealing with here—these drones, the machine learning models—it's cutting-edge stuff. That's why we're running trials. Just wrap up the work, and we'll see how it pans out in the fields."

Garrett rocked on his feet, clearly uncomfortable.

"Put Stella's update in," Martin suggested. "We can test it in the fields."

Garrett nodded, but his mind was churning. When he first got into AI, he'd seen it as the ultimate problem-solver—a tool to streamline processes, eliminate the mundane, and make life simpler. But this project forced him to confront a different side of AI: the unknown variables, the decisions it could make, and the outcomes no one fully controlled.

Now when Garrett used AI, the code wasn't just about making things easier anymore. Every line of code he wrote, every adjustment to the model, carried risks he hadn't considered before. AI was like a live wire, sparking with potential but unpredictable, something that didn't always behave the way he expected. And living things could get hurt.

As Martin talked, Garrett realized he'd been pushing himself to prove he could handle it all, that he could master this technology without help. But now, he felt a new discomfort creeping in, a sense that AI was larger than him, more complex and slippery. Realizing he was in over his head was unsettling.

"The code doesn't have to be perfect," Garrett reminded himself. All he had to do was get through the week so he could return to his university sandbox where the stakes were much lower. And maybe, just maybe, he'd be able to walk away from this internship with a sense of pride and the reference he needed to keep building his future.

"OK," Garrett said out loud. "Next week, after I leave, you'll run the trials with Stella's code in place."

As Garrett turned away, Martin was already strategizing, envisioning how he'd guide the project forward, his name front and center. Martin was sketching out his plans for the next phase of the project. He saw himself taking the helm, free from the hesitations of an eager but inexperienced intern. Martin was thinking about the bigger picture: the meetings he'd schedule, the metrics he'd present, the expansion he'd propose. Garrett got the project off the ground, no doubt, but Martin was the one who'd see it through. He'd be the one leading the conversations with management, talking numbers, piquing their interest, and securing the resources to expand the trial. In Martin's mind, this project was becoming his own, his ticket to the recognition he'd been working toward for years before he had given up. He was energized and back on track.

Chapter 21

Martin looked and smelled like a man who had slept in his clothing—and to be fair, he had. The faint, sour tang of sweat and yesterday's coffee clung to him, a reluctant aura of someone who had been in too many places for too long without a proper break. His appearance wasn't a statement—it was collateral damage from living in his own head.

He reached for his coffee cup, now empty, and stared into it as if willing caffeine residue to materialize into something useful.

Martin rubbed his chin, his gaze fixed on the latest field reports, the cause of his angst. The original trials with Garrett's code had mostly gone to plan, aside from that one unexpected collision. The kangaroos had been effectively driven out, clearing the fields, and the buzz around the project was building. He'd even started receiving nods from management and hints about expanded budgets. There were whispers of bigger things, and, for the first time, murmurs of a promotion. He could have a real office, walls, a door. He could already picture it, a space where he could close out the incessant hum of cubicle neighbors and the chatter of interns who thought they knew everything.

But then Stella's latest code updates arrived, full of safety protocols meant to "minimize risk." She'd called it a necessary adjustment, cautioning that the drones' "aggressive deterrence" behavior could harm wildlife and even people if something went wrong. Reluctantly, Martin had let Garrett implement the new protocols. The project, he figured, couldn't afford another kangaroo collision. Yet the next trial was a setback. The drones hesitated, their responses dulled by the "precautionary measures." The deterrence was less effective because the drones didn't pursue the intruders as quickly or consistently. Weeks of progress seemed to have evaporated overnight.

Martin tapped his fingers on the desk, his jaw clenched. This wasn't just an inconvenience; it threatened the entire project timeline, the results he'd promised to management, and, worst of all, his ascent up the office hierarchy. He needed results. Now.

He picked up the phone and dialed an external consultant recommended by a manager who knew how to get things done. With his increased budget, he could afford to hire someone experienced. This contractor had a reputation for speed. When the consultant arrived later that week, Martin didn't waste any time.

"Just put it back to before the update," Martin said, his voice low. "Those adjustments are holding us up. Drones need to be in full deterrence mode." His tone was firm, his impatience plain.

The consultant nodded, unfazed. This was familiar territory. Companies brought him in to sidestep red tape and get results. "Understood. I'll revert the recent changes," he confirmed. "I'll also deactivate Garrett's access. The last thing you need is surprise updates."

Martin's eyes narrowed with approval. "I need those drones going full tilt. This project's got to hit the mark, or it's done for. And if we nail this, if we can prove it works, we won't just be saving crops." He leaned in, his voice dropping to a whisper, eyes gleaming as he imagined the wider reach. Control over land, livestock, and maybe more.

The consultant implemented the changes, quietly disabled Garrett's account, and the drones were back to their aggressive deterrence mode. The tests showed immediate improvement. The drones chased off intruders, responding faster and with a new autonomy. Martin watched the metrics, the numbers climbing in his favor. It felt good, powerful, even, to know that he alone was steering this project now, without Garrett's cautious hand at the wheel.

Martin packed up for the weekend, shutting down his computer with a feeling of accomplishment. He'd done what was necessary and made the hard call. This was the kind of leadership management wanted: decisive and outcome-focused. As he walked out of the building, he could practically feel that office key in his hand, the door to his future just within reach.

He didn't look back, didn't second-guess the choices he'd made. He had no idea that Alice's project was set up to include all of his project's code automatically. In his haste to push his project forward, he had updated her project as well as any other projects connected to hers.

Chapter 22

Jim Hart was a staunch man who wore a military cut and prided himself on pragmatism. He valued the elegance of a single, sensible solution—a clean break, a solid yes or no. He'd built his security business and career on that principle. But there was no manual, no standard operating procedure for goose removal in security—especially not when the complaint came directly from a billionaire CEO, his longest-standing client, Bill Meyer.

Bill's latest obsession was a flock of Canadian geese that had taken to sunning themselves on his otherwise pristine Rockport estate, occupying his emerald lawn as if they had a share of his legacy. The problem with geese, Bill had barked over the phone, was their stubborn entitlement. "Like any bad employee," he snarled, "they refuse to leave when they're no longer wanted."

Jim didn't care for metaphors; he preferred instructions. What he did know was that Bill was dead serious and that his money kept Jim's business alive. Geese, it seemed, had now officially entered the spectrum of high-priority threats he was expected to handle.

In a stroke of either divine favor or digital coincidence, one of Jim's new hires, Marla—known for her fast fingers and sharp instincts—discovered an intriguing open-source project. A system called

"The Penguin Games," developed by AI scientist Stella Everdeen, was originally designed to monitor and manage colonies of emperor penguins. A programmer named Alice Chen had modified and branched it to deter crows, which, as it turned out, shared a crucial trait with the average goose: they traveled in packs and were surprisingly resistant to moving once they had claimed an inch of territory.

Marla copied Alice Chen's modified code, reprogramming the algorithms to detect and displace Bill's unwanted geese. She commented out the air horn code, removing the rock music sounds, guessing that Axl Rose would be as unwelcome to Bill as the geese themselves. Marla loaded the software onto repurposed drones—sleek, black, and polished, a line item added just last quarter—to patrol Bill's acreage on autopilot. Each bird was tracked, flagged, and, well, chased.

That might have been the end of it, except Bill had other properties. Bill demanded that the Rockport experiment—now called the "Bird Deterrence Protocol"—be replicated across every square inch of all his estates. In Palm Springs, the drones were programmed to deter desert quail. In Newport Rhode Island, on his Ocean Drive waterfront mansion which bordered the famous Cliff Walks, they targeted seagulls.

Jim found himself not only defending Bill's land from potential intruders, but managing a growing portfolio of avian hostilities. It wasn't what he had imagined, years ago, fresh out of military service. But it was his job now and it paid the bills.

Pragmatism had always been Jim's strongest asset.

Chapter 23

Stella moved through her house, the hum of excitement buzzing under her skin as if her bones had already set sail while she was still packing. Finnick padded at her heels, his big, soulful eyes fixed on her every move, sensing that something unusual was afoot. He stuck close to her side, nudging his nose into her duffel bag as if to say, "Take me with you."

"Not this time, buddy," she murmured, scratching behind his ears. "This is a trip for humans only."

Finnick whined softly, plopping down next to her half-packed bags, his eyes following her as she made her way back and forth between her closet and the gear spread out across her bed. It held her parka, a set of extra-thick long johns, wool socks, and tubes of Vaseline to coat her exposed skin against the harsh winds of Antarctica. The parka was high-tech, a deep forest green with multiple layers, designed to trap heat even in the coldest environments. It had taken her months to find the right one, and now she ran her fingers over it, savoring the moment. She couldn't believe it; she was going. This was the trip of a lifetime, her dream taking shape in the duffel bags and sturdy cases stacked around her.

Her fingers grazed the handle of her laptop, and she felt a gentle tug of reality pulling her back from the frozen landscapes she was dreaming about. There was still work to finish. One last check, one final test. She'd run through the code so many times that she could almost do it in her sleep, but this wasn't just another trial. This was the final check before she packed up her laptop for good. She couldn't afford any surprises when she was out there in the snow.

She flipped her laptop open and navigated to the program. The code was working in a closed loop, designed to process still images from the cameras and send them back to the local servers she'd configured specifically for this trip. The program was self-contained, ready to function without Internet access in the remote wilderness. Once the cameras captured their images, the data would feed directly into LAT's servers whenever they had a satellite connection, uploading to the cloud for further analysis.

The entire system would be practically autonomous. All she'd need her laptop for was to address any minor local issues and tweak the image analysis as they encountered real-world variables she couldn't predict from her living room. She could almost see it now: the cameras rolling, the pristine white landscape dotted with clusters of penguins, each one identified, cataloged, their unique markings preserved in a digital record for research teams back home. She felt her breath catch at the thought.

She sat down at her desk and glanced at a neatly folded stack of papers, her project outline, full of technical details, with pages upon pages about data flow and autonomous systems. The management team at LAT had been enthralled when she'd presented it to them last week. She remembered their faces, wide-eyed and leaning forward, captivated by the potential.

Their interest had only intensified when she'd discussed the possibilities of integrating drone footage. The drones could cover vast swaths of terrain she'd never dreamed of reaching. It was Violet who'd sparked the initial idea after showing her some of the footage Garrett's team had sent from Australia. The Agriculture and Trade Bureau's code base was solid, and Stella had been careful to integrate it seamlessly, testing and running spot checks to make sure it didn't disrupt her existing system. Eager to support the expansion, LAT offered to supply ruggedized drones built for extreme conditions. And National Scientific had practically cheered when she shared the plans.

"Almost there," she whispered, running one last code pull and diagnostic. Her code was the main branch, and as such she did not receive or see the update Martin had recently made and pushed back to his branch. Not everyone would be so lucky. The system blinked back at her, a confirmation of compile success. She felt a thrill of satisfaction. Every part of the project was ready.

She fired off a quick message to Violet, telling her to hold down the fort.

Violet pinged back a moment later.
Violet: Safe travels, boss. Antarctica better be ready for you.

Stella smiled and sent a quick reply. Her thoughts drifted to the logistics. Her servers would be boxed and shipped to the airport tonight, waiting for her in Chile next week. There, they'd be loaded onto the vessel bound for the frozen continent where, among the ice and the wild, her vision would come to life. She was ready to step onto her seventh continent at last.

Packing away her laptop, she shivered with excitement. This was it. This was her moment.

"Come on Finnick, let's get you over to Alice's," Stella said to her pup. Finnick was at her side in an instant, ready and eager for a field walk. It was a beautiful spring day, and Stella left her jacket on the rack.

Chapter 24

Spring was stretching its limbs across the fields, coaxing green buds from the earth, awakening the bees to their persistent buzz. The air held that subtle warmth, just enough to hint at the life stirring beneath the soil. Alice leaned back in her chair, cradling her coffee, letting her gaze wander lazily over the emails filling her screen. Between her work and managing the drones, she was usually too busy to savor mornings like this, but today, the sunlight streaming in and the scent of damp earth felt grounding.

A soft chime pulled her attention to her phone. It was a message from Stella, who was in the midst of a whirlwind of last-minute packing for her long-awaited trip to Antarctica.

Stella: Thanks again for watching Finnick while I'm gone. Walking him over now. Appreciate it more than you know.

Alice smiled at the message, picturing Stella trekking through the familiar trails with Finnick trotting alongside her, his tail wagging as he explored every nook and cranny. Alice was looking forward to dog-sitting, especially after how helpful Stella's updates had been in keeping her fields crow-free. With the latest patches, the drones had stopped behaving unpredictably. Paul, her husband, hadn't noticed any issues either, so she felt reassured, maybe even a bit proud that the system was working.

As she took another sip of coffee, her computer chimed with a familiar notification. She glanced at it. A drone alert. One of the regular reports that had become part of her daily routine. "Repeat offender detected," the screen read, along with the name her algorithm had assigned: Russell Crowe.

She snorted at the name, half amused, half annoyed. Then she paused.

"Repeat offender" was the old alert. The one before Stella fixed the code. She'd almost dismissed it, her thoughts more on Stella's departure than anything else. But curiosity nudged her hand toward the mouse, and she clicked on the link to the live feed.

The screen flickered, and the drones' cameras adjusted, bringing the landscape into sharp focus. Sunlight spilled over the fields, casting long shadows over the rows of freshly turned soil. But what caught her eye wasn't an intruding pest. Instead, her breath hitched as she took in the unmistakable figure at the edge of her field.

Finnick.

Her pulse quickened as she watched, confusion and dread tightening in her chest. Finnick wasn't alone. The drones, her drones, were closing in on him, their movements purposeful, almost predatory, circling him like he was a marked target. She could see him dart left, then right, evading the relentless pursuit, his ears flat, tail tucked low. Panic flared in his eyes. And right beside him, Stella swatted at the drones. Alice saw Stella run off the field toward the woods.

Alice's heart leaped into her throat. Her fingers flew to the keyboard, immediately executing the emergency shutdown. With a few swift keystrokes, she sent the kill command, forcing each drone to drop from the sky, halting their pursuit in an instant. But the sinking feeling remained. She slammed her laptop shut, bolting out the door without a second thought, unaware of the coffee spilling across her desk.

The spring air slapped her cheeks as she sprinted toward the fields. Her boots hit the earth in uneven strides, stumbling over roots and rocks as her thoughts raced faster than her feet.

"Finnick!" she called, her voice cracking with urgency. Her legs burned as she pushed herself harder, her vision blurring with panic. She didn't want to believe what she'd just seen. Finnick was family, Stella's beloved companion, and the idea that her creation had turned against him felt like a betrayal.

As she neared them, she froze. The drones were haphazardly strewn across the ground, their propellers tangled in the dirt, still as fallen leaves.

And then, just beyond them, her gaze locked onto Finnick. And a figure lying crumpled among the foliage.

Stella.

Alice's heart plummeted as she rushed forward, her mind grappling with the scene. Finnick was pawing frantically at Stella, his whines sharp and desperate. She could see the swell of red marks across Stella's skin, angry welts dotting her face and arms. Bee stings. Swarming around them were the remnants of disturbed hives, the angry buzz of bees filling the air, furious at being jolted from their peace.

What had just happened clicked together in Alice's mind, each piece falling into place with chilling clarity. The drones hadn't just pursued Finnick. They had pushed Stella across the field into the woods and herded her until she stumbled into the hives. The technology that was meant to safeguard Alice's fields had become something she couldn't control.

Alice knelt beside Stella, her hands shaking as she reached for her friend, praying that she wasn't too late. In that instant, the boundaries between creator and creation, between intention and consequence, collapsed, leaving only the harrowing truth of what had gone wrong.

"Her EpiPen," Alice said frantically. "She's never without her mace and EpiPen."

Alice started searching Stella's pockets. Empty. Hands shaking, Alice dialed 911.

Stella's death barely made a ripple. A short obituary in the local paper, a heartfelt post on LinkedIn from her boss, a few reactions and condolences from her colleagues, and life carried on. The team at National Scientific team loaded the ship and sailed without Stella.

Chapter 25

Violet attended Stella's service, standing quietly at the back as the small gathering paid their respects. She didn't cry. She didn't speak. Public displays of emotion had no place in her tightly controlled psyche. She had spent years perfecting the art of keeping her feelings in check, compartmentalizing grief into neat, orderly spaces where it couldn't disrupt her focus.

After the service, Violet returned to her work, her outward demeanor unchanged. But inside, a familiar unease churned. The open-source project she'd worked so hard to launch had taken on a life of its own, and for the first time, she felt its weight as a responsibility rather than an accomplishment. Stella's death was a stark reminder that code wasn't neutral, that even the best intentions could pave the way for unintended consequences.

Alice sat in her kitchen, staring at her coffee mug as the steam curled into the air. The silence in the house was deafening, punctuated only by the occasional creak of floorboards. She'd done what she thought was right—publishing a frank, unvarnished account of the drones, the dangers of unchecked open-source AI, and the decisions that had led to Stella's death. She'd laid it all bare, from the initial enthusiasm to the oversight that turned fatal.

The post barely made a ripple. Thirty "Support" reactions, no comments of significance, and certainly no visits from regulators or lawyers. Alice had expected a storm, a reckoning. Instead, there was silence.

She let out a bitter laugh, the sound echoing in the empty room. When you're a farmer, no one pays attention to your social media posts.

Alice pushed the mug aside and opened her laptop. There was no undoing what had happened, no erasing the guilt that lingered in the corners of her mind. But if her words saved even one life, even one more tragedy, then perhaps it was worth it. She glanced at the empty fields outside her window, the wind stirring the dry stalks, and wondered if this was what accountability felt like—heavy, quiet, and unresolved.

Garrett had logged into LinkedIn on the long plane ride home. He was one of the people who read Alice's post. He had a gut-wrenching feeling. What had he done? He logged into his GitHub to try to unravel what had happened. He was locked out of editing the project. A slow, creeping awareness of what had happened grew as he dug through the code logs. The rollback of Stella's updates hadn't been his decision. He hadn't even been informed. And when he found the changes—when he traced the deletion of safety protocols back to Martin's account—Garrett felt a deep, sinking weight in his chest. The program, the one he'd poured himself into, had been compromised in ways he couldn't ethically ignore.

During the long, sleepless flight and countless cups of bad coffee, he decided what to do. Reporting Martin wasn't just about calling out his former manager—it was about stopping something that had spiraled out of control. He knew what it could cost him his recommendation, maybe even his future in the industry. But he also knew he couldn't stay silent.

Garrett filed a report directly with the Agriculture and Trade Bureau leadership, outlining the changes to the code, the risks they introduced, and the incident with the drones. He included everything—his concerns, his misgivings, and his new belief that AI needed to serve humans responsibly, not recklessly. He detailed how the rollback had led to a lack of control.

Garrett felt defeated but also, strangely, proud. As the plane carried him back to the Midwest, Garrett made a quiet promise to himself: he'd focus on the ethical ramifications of AI. This wasn't the end of his journey—just a redirection.

The program was shut down within days. Garrett received an email thanking him for his honesty and reminding him of his Non-Disclosure Agreement. The language was polite but unyielding. He was being told to keep quiet.

Martin, meanwhile, sat in his cubical. The fallout from the report had been swift. His promotion prospects evaporated overnight. The whispers about an office with walls and a door? Gone. The only thing he had left was his cubicle with its small, narrow window.

He found himself staring out of it more often than not, the sunlight filtering through and highlighting the fine layer of dust on his desk. The window had always been a consolation prize, a small indicator that he was just a little more important than those without one. Now it felt like a reminder of what he'd lost. His gamble to fast-track the project and cut corners had cost him not just his professional reputation but also the chance to build something meaningful.

Martin sighed, leaning back in his chair. He could still hear Garrett's voice in his head, cautious and questioning, pointing out the flaws in the system Martin had been so eager to overlook. Garrett shook his head, pushing the thoughts aside. Regret wasn't something he allowed himself often, but today, it felt unavoidable.

Epilogue

The morning sun rose over the Atlantic, casting a gentle light over the Cliff Walk in Newport. A lone jogger and his shepherd mix made their way along the trail that lined the cliffs, the dog darting up the lawns of the mansions along the path. The shepherd sniffed through the brambles and undergrowth sussing out the new day's scents. The man, a retired software engineer named Harold, smiled as he watched his dog run ahead on the lawns of the private mansions, the early chill from the breeze off the ocean bringing a flush to his cheeks.

He had taken this path hundreds of times, its turns and vistas as familiar to him as the rhythm of his breath. The beautiful cliff is on one side, and the lawns and mansions are on the other. It was good for the soul. But as he rounded a bend in the trail, he heard a faint buzzing in the distance. A sound that had no place among the birdsong and the crashing waves. He stopped, frowning, scanning for its source.

The dog, oblivious, continued his playful romp, barking at a shadow that flickered over the undergrowth. A dark shape hovered above him, now clearly a mechanical hum slicing through the quiet morning air. Harold squinted, shading his eyes against the sun's glare. It was a drone, small but sleek, its movements precise and deliberate as it hovered, circling.

Harold shook his head, growling under his breath about tourists and their gadgets. He turned away, calling his dog back to his side. But the buzzing grew louder, more insistent, a high-pitched whine that seemed to echo against the rocks. He glanced back, his irritation giving way to unease as the drone swept lower, its camera lens fixed on him and his dog.

The dog barked again, leaping up at the approaching drone, and Harold's unease turned to anger. "Hey! Get!" he shouted, waving his hands to shoo it away. But the drone ignored him, its trajectory shifting to follow the dog's frantic movements.

A chill ran down Harold's spine. This wasn't just a hobbyist's toy. The drone was behaving with a purpose—pushing, following. It moved with the precision of a hunter, adjusting its position each time the dog darted left or right.

He reached out, trying to grab the drone out of the air, but it swooped back, its movements unnaturally quick. As Harold stumbled forward, he tripped over an exposed root, sprawling onto the ground. He barely had time to regain his footing when the drone dipped lower again, sending the dog into a frenzy.

Harold's hands swatted at the air as he cried out, stumbling backward. The last thing Harold saw before falling over the cliff was the drone's unblinking eye.

The news of Harold's death made the rounds in local papers, filed under "Unfortunate Hiking Accident." The cause of death was listed as a fall from the cliff, resulting in blunt force trauma to the head and drowning in the sea. His family, grief-stricken, requested privacy as they buried him in the town cemetery, his dog by their side, the animal's eyes searching for its lost companion.

No one connected the dots. No one looked for the drone that was trained to keep seagulls off of Bill Meyer's lawn. No one noticed the similarities to another incident, a mere 100 miles away, where a drone had malfunctioned, setting off a chain of events that ended in Stella Everdeen's death.

But somewhere, in the code bases of anonymous developers, a pattern began to form—an algorithm behaving as its creators coded, and in ways no one had foreseen. And as the drones continued to fly over fields, over snow, over forests and beaches, the hum of their engines carried with them a question that no one had yet dared to ask: What else had they been programmed to do?

Acknowledgments

To my family - always.

Thank you to Debra Slapak, Roseanne Ouellette, AnnMarie Reyes Harvie, and Vin Femia for their thoughtful feedback and support.

Made in United States
North Haven, CT
12 January 2025